THE
SWEET
SPOT

Also by Peter C. Cavelti

How To Invest In Gold
McClelland & Stewart, Toronto and Follett Publishing, Chicago

Gold, Silver & Strategic Metals
McClelland & Stewart, Toronto and McGraw Hill, New York

Tuiavii's Way: A South Sea Chief's Comments on Western Society
Legacy Editions, Toronto and Sanseido, Tokyo

A Dangerous Remedy
Legacy Editions, Toronto

Moments In Time: The Experience of My Life
A Memoir in three Volumes
Legacy Editions, Toronto and Ingram Sparks, La Vergne

Thoughtful Giving: A Journey Through the Charitable Universe
Legacy Editions, Toronto and Ingram Sparks, La Vergne

THE SWEET SPOT

A Novel

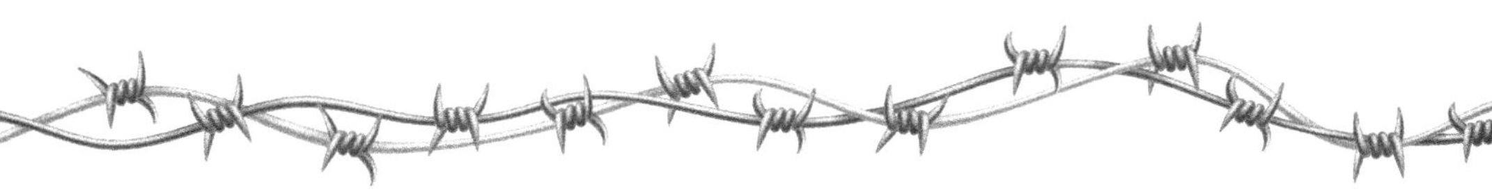

PETER CAVELTI

LIBRARY AND ARCHIVES OF CANADA
Cavelti, Peter C. (Peter Christian), 1948–
The Sweet Spot
Legacy Editions
ISBN 978-1-7780316-8-7 (print)   ISBN 978-1-7780316-9-4 (ebook)

Content Design: Laura Brady
Cover Design: Michel Vrana

Printed in the United States of America

For Caroline

And In Loving Memory of Krista and Gaby

1

HE STARES AHEAD AS THE stainless-steel doors softly slide together. He's done his job and he's no longer at work. Closure. Jack Grayson thinks of the elevator as a twilight zone, the way other people do of the train that carries them home.

He turns his head and watches himself in the spotless mirror. A smile touches his lips and throws wrinkles to the sides of his eyes. The extra mile. It's all paying off. He takes in the expensive suit, the impeccably knotted tie, his shoes reflecting the light from the recessed halogen bulbs overhead. Grayson has no complaints.

As elevator rides go this one takes its time, but he doesn't mind. Apart from the sensation he always feels when the doors close, he also likes the way the cab slows down for a stop. Soft as a feather, accompanied by an almost imperceptible whoosh. Today the elevator stops twice in the 50s and then again on 34, where the Fedex driver steps in.

Grayson sees him only from behind, but he notices the man's wavy silver hair and tanned neck, a tattoo disappearing into the collar of his uniform. The curved end of an anchor or a whale's fin?

Grayson's eyes come to rest on the hand that holds an over-sized envelope: strong, with conspicuously well-kept nails. Grayson wonders what twist of fate has made the fellow a Fedex driver. Probably an immigrant, he muses. First generation. With a Maltese degree in economics. He reconsiders. Maybe the man is simply unambitious.

On his way to the car Grayson reflects on how well everything has worked out. By putting in an extra hour or two each day and staying with the company, he's moved far beyond where he should logically be. It's simple: most others have fallen behind because they've insisted on driving their kids to hockey practice or catching the five o'clock train at Union Station.

He crosses Wellington Street. The most unexpected thing is that nothing's suffered at home. Some of his colleagues are stuck in destructive marriages; others have cut their losses and moved on. And of those few who have a wife they can relate to, most have problems with their kids. Teenagers running off to Montreal or New York, drugs, pregnancies.

He remembers talking to Marlene when she was pregnant, telling her to stop worrying about cleaning or gardening. Ever since, her task has been to be there for the kids and his to bring in the money. That's the key to their success. A shared sense of mission.

An image from last year's trip to Morocco crowds in. Marlene and the boys are standing next to Ayoub, their guide, who's telling them what to expect, while an elderly handler leads five camels toward them. A few palm trees mark the edge of the desert, but a bit further out, the way they will soon be headed, monotonous barren dunes as far as the eye can see.

He hears Ayoub's high-pitched voice again, this time explaining that it's important to approach a camel from the side and earn its trust. Stand next to it for a few moments; if you want to, gently touch the back of its neck. And then, when the handler tells you to, you can mount.

Oliver, soon to be eleven, is finding it difficult to wait. He's excited and still in disbelief that he and his kid brother will each have their own animal. And behind him stands Martin, seeking out his parents' eyes, looking for reassurance.

Next, Grayson contemplates the fragile figures of the boys ahead of them, perched on top of the gently swaying camels, the blue headscarves they've been given blending into the uncompromising, cloudless sky. And then Grayson turns to look at Marlene who's riding next to him, and he notices something he hasn't seen for a while: her face radiates purest joy. No, more than that—exhilaration.

The four of them on an adventure, building memories. Another few years and the boys will be adults, but what they've shared today will stay with them a lifetime!

Grayson suddenly feels hot. He wonders whether it's because of Toronto's July weather or his memories.

At the parking lot the attendant steps out of his booth, interrupting his thoughts. "I got it washed like you wanted, Mr. Grayson. The keys are inside."

"Thanks Miguel." He knows the man's name, even remembers that he's from Honduras. He's looked after the lot forever.

Grayson takes off his jacket and admires the immaculate green hood of his Lexus reflecting the office towers above him. The rounded metal distorts their shape, yet the lines are razor sharp. Then he lets himself slide into the lavish interior. He turns the key and the dashboard in front of him comes alive, a softly lit array of knobs and dials. His to command.

Traffic has died down, another thing he loves about his routine.

An hour from now the downtown canyons will start to fill up again, as people head for restaurants, shows and sports events. But now the downtown streets are almost empty. He thinks of it as a sweet spot.

Come to think of it, his whole life will soon enter a sweet spot. The boys will be at boarding school and he and Marlene will have more time together. And if all goes right, he'll be elected to the board of directors this summer. He'll take her to London to celebrate. They'll go for walks in St. James's Park, just like they did on their honeymoon.

Grayson notices the orange light below his speedometer. A flicker of irritation crosses his brow, then he remembers the gas station near the bus terminal. It's a 24-hour self-serve.

He keeps pushing the green plastic tab saying PREMIUM, but nothing happens. He looks around for someone to ask, but he's alone. Then he slowly reads the instructions and grins. Sometimes it's good to do ordinary things. Keeps you in touch with regular life. The pump starts to hum.

Grayson is surprised by how fast the digital numbers race by, yet how long it takes to fill his tank. The smell bothers him. He notices a black van at the side of the building. It must have been there when he arrived, otherwise he would have noticed it pulling up. A plume of bluish exhaust comes from its tailpipe, but no one is inside.

As Grayson turns back to the pump, a gush of gasoline spews out of the tank and down the side of his car. "Shit, I thought this type of thing wasn't supposed to happen," he says aloud. He checks his pants and shoes, but they're fine. Only his right hand is wet. He puts the nozzle back into its slot and pulls out his handkerchief. But the gas has already evaporated. A dry white film reaches down his palm and the sides of his fingers. He'll need to wash it off or his car will smell for days.

Grayson hears a dull plop coming from the direction of the pay booth, then another. He looks over, but there's nothing.

He leans into his car, reaching over to the passenger seat to fish the wallet from his jacket. He emerges, pushes the car door shut and turns. Two tall men are walking toward him.

One of them is talking, nodding at Grayson. He looks agitated. Grayson can't hear—he just sees the man's jaw move. Then the other, a fellow with cropped light hair, reaches into his jacket. When Grayson sees the pistol, he doesn't know what to do. He just stands there, holding his wallet.

For a while Grayson floats on his belly, looking down. On the ground below he sees flashing lights and a throng of people standing around the spread-out form of a human, the white shirt like a beacon against the harsh, oil-stained pavement between the red-and-white pumps. In time he realizes the form belonged to him, *was him,* and that makes him look at it more closely. How benign it seems in its lifelessness, how irrelevant. He wonders why it attracts such attention, but he doesn't let it bother him. All he feels is relief that he can now do without it and gratitude that it served him well.

A voice then, but one without any sound attached to it. More than a voice, he realizes—a deep and overwhelming knowing that makes him comprehend that all here is love, that there is nothing but love. Gradually, he opens himself to the embrace of such benevolence and marvels at the soothing light that surrounds him.

He sees people he knows. There's Uncle Drew, wearing a hat with earflaps on the side and a checkered woolen shirt, except he's beardless now. And Cousin Helen, whom he hasn't seen since before her accident. It must be thirty years ago, but her freckles are still there, and bangs cover her forehead the way they always have. Helen, bathed in an impossibly warm glow, is wearing a flowery summer dress.

His grandparents are there too, welcoming him with the broadest imaginable smiles. "My sweet Jack," Grandma says, radiating goodness. What he wants most is to go to her and rest his head against her belly and feel her arms closing around him, but he knows both he and grandma have no need for their bodies. They're floating, absorbing each other's love and projecting their limitless acceptance of all.

For a long time, Grayson dwells in this state of infinite grace, immersing himself in its truthful radiance.

As he journeys on, he notices a change in the light. And he wonders where Marlene and the boys are. But something urges him to let go of the unease of that thought, assuring him that all is well. His loved ones will be fine; they no longer need him.

For a while longer, Grayson allows himself to be cuddled by the promise of eternal perfection, but then discomfort about his family rises once more and he decides it's time to leave.

The figures lining the wall become denser and less radiant. Mr. Bopp, his grade-school teacher, is dressed in a dark suit and looks curiously fleshy. Next to him stands Anne Gramercy, their neighbor, holding out a cone to him. The two impeccably arranged purple scoops absorb Jack and he decides to stay and contemplate them. But something makes him raise his eyes, and when he looks up at Mrs. Gramercy he knows something is very wrong. Her face is pasty and bloated and beads of sweat cover her forehead.

Then pain. Not sharp or definable, but leaden and all over. As if the weight of the world had been placed on his chest and its burden had spread to every one of his bones.

Now Grayson is outside his parents' house. He's hovering somewhere over the garden trying to orient himself by the flowerbeds, but he can't make them out. The night is like wet pitch. He feels confused and nauseous.

Eventually, he sees the dim bulb over the kitchen sink and even though he can't see his mother he knows she's there inside, leaning forward over the dinner dishes, her profuse grey hair an impenetrable veil covering her eyes. He reaches up to tap on the window and that draws a dozen knives deep into his back. Grayson cringes in agony and wants to vomit but his stomach is empty as a withered party balloon. All he can manage is a series of dismal retches.

When they subside he tries again, managing to reach higher and tap the glass. This time the knives feel dull-bladed and viciously serrated as they fumble their way around inside his spine. He presses his eyes shut, not even noticing the satanic shower of exploding lights behind his lids, grits his teeth until the back of his head hurts so much it brings back the retching.

Much later, when the pain ebbs off and his stomach stops convulsing, Grayson hears the groan of the heavy front door, and he knows it's Mom even before he sees the blurred outline against the flood of light behind her. His heartbeat quickens as he strains to scan her expression, get even a fleeting look at her eyes, and fails. He's too far away.

Then Mom tilts her head, almost unnoticeably, and he takes this as a sign to approach. He rushes toward her, buoyed by anticipation, expecting her arms to open and her embrace to tell him he's forgiven. But as he gets close Mom lowers her eyes and stiffens and his hope crumbles. He knows what's coming. She'll turn to climb the stairs. She'll take him to the tower.

Grayson sees a streak of blond hair. Marlene! Is this the night she's come to his room, his parents asleep downstairs? No, this is not Marlene the girl, but Marlene his wife. He knows because he smells L'Air du Temps, the perfume he brings her when he comes back from Europe.

Somewhere in the room people whisper. The voices are unfamiliar, the words indistinguishable. Grayson doesn't mind. He finds their trivial lilt soothing. A cocoon spun of syllables in which he can rest.

Later, when Marlene lifts her head he can see her face, a mess of tears and exhaustion. Behind her he sees the foot of what is to be his bed for weeks to come. He remembers being caught in the vise of an ache so all-encompassing and that makes him want to ask why there is no pain now.

Grayson's drugged mind makes his lips form the question, contemplates what it would sound like. But when he reopens his eyes, he can tell Marlene hasn't noticed he's awake. He decides to slip back into the safety of nothingness.

2

IMAGINE A WINTER DAY IN a resort town. Oversized cars with out-of-state license plates crawl clumsily through the narrow darkening streets, occasionally skidding on a patch of ice or softly bouncing off a snowbank. Moving along on foot are visitors from Chicago, Houston and Los Angeles, as well as some from distant continents and a few who live and work here.

The locals are easy to spot. They look ordinary, are practically dressed and their movements are driven by purpose. The tourists are equally unmistakable. Some rush along as if they were on a critical mission, trying hard to look stylishly adventurous, but not quite managing. Others look lost, their expressions timid and their steps uncertain, as though they weren't worthy of visiting here. And then there are those who've been attired by the nearby boutiques, exotic mirages trying to blend into a small town that without them would be sentenced to utter ordinariness, wind-up toys painted and glossed to perfection and handicapped only by their scripted movements. Some are elegant and others gaudy, but they all walk along mechanically, cautious not to give the smooth soles of their dress boots reason to slip and determined not to miss anything in the festively lit shop windows.

One of those windows belongs to a café, inside of which sits its owner, Ros Dexter. She nervously leafs through the auto section of the Aspen Daily News and mutters, "Not that I need a bloody car—or could afford one." She tosses the paper aside.

"You look unhappy," says Jack Grayson, who sits at the table next to hers. He's leaning firmly back into his chair, which rests on only two legs and is at risk of tipping.

Ros looks up at him but doesn't answer.

"Why?" he probes.

"You don't want to know."

"Come on, kid. I thought we were friends."

"Right, I forgot. I look after you when you're not hiding in your castle."

"Look Ros, don't take this out on me. I'm trying to help." Grayson hears the edge to his voice and reminds himself to stay cool.

But Ros backs off, apologizing. They look at each other, taking in what just happened.

Then Grayson says, "When you're emotional your Australian accent takes over. And mannerism." He's pleased that his words sound playful.

"And what's that like?"

"Edgy. Don't come near me now."

Ros shrugs and puts on an air of surprise.

He offers, "Why don't you get yourself another cappuccino and sit with me? We can talk." But Ros ignores the suggestion. Grayson rocks his chair, watching her pick up a sugar package and pour its contents into her almost empty cup, then take her spoon and stab it at the brown mess.

After a while Ros gets up and starts walking towards the counter, but halfway there she hesitates. She turns back to Grayson, sits down next to him and tells him about her morning. How she's gone through her mail, munching on almonds, and cracked a crown. And then, opening an envelope from her landlord, found out that she'd lose her apartment.

Grayson says he's sorry and Ros shrugs sadly. "And how's your leg?" she asks.

"No worse than usual. No better, either."

They look at each other, their faces a mix of resignation and comfort in having each other. Grayson suggests they have dinner together.

"What's that going to do? You've already forgotten I can't eat properly."

Grayson waits.

"Only if it costs less than twenty bucks," she says.

"I don't know places like that, so you'll have to show me the way."

Strings of colorful lights glow above them and Mexican music blares from badly made speakers. The waiter asks if they want more drinks. Ros says she needs another Margarita and Grayson orders more Diet Coke. The cheerfulness of the restaurant contrasts with the pace of their conversation.

"You're still looking gloomy," Grayson tries again.

"And why would I feel better?" she shoots back.

"The Margaritas, maybe," he offers dryly and finally Ros grins.

"Tell me Grayson, what's a bad day like for you? When the stock market drops?"

"Don't be snarky. I can help you with your apartment and if you want, with your teeth. But to chase your blues away..."

"I'm usually more cheery," Ros says.

"Cheeriest person in town."

"Okay, so I have my moods." She giggles. "Doesn't everyone?"

"Maybe."

"Anyway, Grayson, what's this interest in my wellbeing?"

"I can see you're going through a rough spot. And we both live in a small town."

"Strikingly different parts of town."

"Don't be difficult, Ros. We won't let that come between us, will we?"

She considers.

"Ros, it's me—Jack Grayson. We've known each other for years. We have coffee together, or at least near each other, most mornings. I *am* interested in your wellbeing!"

"Thank you." For a few seconds, Ros looks at him gravely. "Still, why such interest, Grayson? And where's your wife?"

"Off at the spa."

"So you thought you'd take me under your wings until she's back. Is that it?"

"You Aussies. Always on guard, aren't you?"

His thoughts turn to the night he first met Ros. Samantha was away and Grayson took the opportunity to go to a party. He noticed her right away because she was different. Others scurried around, asking people questions without being the least interested in answers, anxious to talk about themselves or move on. Ros was standing by herself: tall, a simple black dress accentuating her slim figure, her sunburnt face ringed by auburn shoulder-length hair. Grayson watched as people walked toward her, then turned away as if they were frightened to step across some imaginary line.

For a while they both stood, observing the mindless swirl of the crowd between them. Then Ros approached him, saying since they were the only loners in the crowd they might as well get to know each other. Her words were light-hearted, but Grayson could sense the tension beneath them. Here was someone who wasn't comfortable with social niceties. Yet despite the intensity Ros projected, Grayson felt at ease. And as they conversed, he began to enjoy her company. She expressed her views intelligently and with sincerity and she never asked what he did for a living. He liked that.

Near the end of the evening the hostess came over and introduced them formally. She described Ros as an important photographer and urged Grayson to see her art. Now he felt badly. They had talked for an hour or more and he'd never thought of asking about her life. But when he noticed Ros' embarrassment about being shown off, he knew it was okay.

Ros pulls him back from his thoughts. "You haven't answered my question," she says, looking up over the rim of her second Margarita.

"Fair enough. What am I doing here with you?" Grayson catches himself not knowing.

"Is it animal attraction or do we have something to discuss?"

"Christ, Ros, what are you interrogating me for? We're here because I want to help you, remember?" A moment ago he felt close to her. Now he's ready to dismiss the evening as a waste. He watches his hand close around a paper napkin and crush it.

She eyes him for a long moment. "I'm sorry, Grayson. I suppose I had to be sure of that."

"Of what?"

"That there is nothing more. When it comes to men my defense barrier is in the stratosphere."

As he has a hundred times before, Grayson notices the unsettling intensity of her eyes. He holds her stare. "I guess you don't get out to dinner a lot," he says, immediately regretting his words.

But Ros lets it go. "Better to stay with safe topics, Grayson."

"Like your cracked crown and losing your apartment?"

Her face relaxes, then turns serious again. "You know a lot about me, Grayson. Maybe that's why I feel vulnerable."

Grayson watches Ros walk away from his car. He knows she's had three Margaritas, but her steps are determined. He thinks it's part of her shell, betting that the real Ros is gently floating toward her front door.

For a few seconds he holds the memory of the hug she's given him just now. Embracing him a bit longer than he expected, but then determinedly pulling back. As he slips his car into gear Grayson decides she likes him but doesn't want to get too close. He wonders if that will keep her from accepting his help.

As he cruises along, his thoughts turn to Samantha and his orchids. How surprised he was this morning when he noticed his favourite, the dark violet one, starting to drive blooms—now, in the middle of winter. His wife, who loves all flowers but absolutely adores orchids, will be so pleased!

With his corporate duties long gone and his physical rehabilitation mostly behind him, Grayson keeps trying to nurture new interests. There is too much empty space in his days, especially when he doesn't ski.

If he had to rank his activities, he'd give his on-mountain time the top mark. Even though his movements are often jerky and he has to stick to the blue runs, gliding down Aspen Mountain gives him the sensation of physical prowess. Nothing beats skiing!

Mornings at the café and dinners with Samantha would be in the enjoyable category, perhaps along with reading. Jogging and gym time would have to be classified as activities he doesn't look forward to, but often enjoys once he gets going. The final column would be devoted to administrative tasks, like keeping on top of his investments, preparing tax returns or dealing with insurance policies—necessary but far from gratifying. Tolerable would be a better word.

Grayson knows that he needs more positive content in his life; looking after his dozen orchids and learning about them is a beginning. This spring, he may even create an outdoor garden. He's already checked into the perennials that would grow best in Aspen's difficult conditions. He smiles at that thought. Before his calamity, his spreadsheets used to track revenue components, expense segments, personnel performance and client statistics. Now his research focuses on growing things. As he contemplates this transition, his brain serves up the images of Siberian sage, catmint and lavender he's downloaded onto his laptop, all in shades of intense purple.

Will he ever be a seasoned gardener? Maybe one day he'll end up lecturing visitors from Europe on how high up and how far South Aspen is. He imagines himself at the café, hears himself talk. "You see, you're 8000 feet above sea level, but you are on the same latitude as Ibiza or Lesbos. Yes, the altitude and the intensity of solar radiation, coupled with the extreme dryness of the air, make growing things here a challenge. But a worthwhile one!"

Traffic is almost non-existent. Even Main Street, usually busy at this hour, is nearly deserted. But as Grayson passes the bakery a Jeep shoots out of the side street, horn blasting and heading straight for him. Grayson hits the brake hard and feels his car swerve. As his tires slam against the curb, he sees the faces of two teenagers pass by, perplexingly slow despite the speed of their vehicle, bluish pale in the beam of his headlights. The girl's face is taut with terror, but her friend at the steering wheel is laughing hysterically. Their car barely misses his, then arcs into Main Street and speeds away.

"I'll kill that little fucker," Grayson swears and floors his accelerator, forgetting that his engine has stalled. His rage explodes and he starts screaming. He restarts his car, lets the engine howl and initiates a U-turn. But he speeds up too soon and loses control. When he comes to a stop his car is half-way on the sidewalk, the engine silent once again.

Grayson stares into the nothingness of his windshield, not sure how long he's been here, his white hands clamped to the steering wheel and his body shaking. The chemical smell he's learned to fear is back and he knows he must clench the steering wheel no matter what, or his hands will disobey him and smash into whatever is in front of them. Not this time, Grayson vows, clinging to reality while acrid tears bite into his eyes.

Gradually, memory takes over—the memory of the endless battle for control of his mind. And with that memory comes the knowledge of what he has to do. Calling forth every bit of concentration, he makes his right hand inch across the wheel to meet the left so that the two hands, each lending strength and guiding the other, can find their way down the side of the door and open the handle.

Outside, he starts to breathe. His temples throb and the taste of bile is thick on his tongue. But he breathes, leaning against the side of his car, much as he leaned against his car at the gas station after being shot. He breathes slowly and deliberately and that helps. And then he imagines himself looking down from above, seeing himself through the soothing drizzle, a mere speck in the small town of Aspen. Looking far into the distance he imagines the taillights of a Jeep speeding down Highway 82, two teenagers inside, irrelevant specks themselves.

How trivial we are, Grayson thinks. And as he contemplates the insignificance of the incident he's lived through, images of a tortured world take over. Scenes of parched fields and burning forests accompany his breathing and then there's war. He watches a group of village women being herded into a barbed wire enclosure, their faces terror-stricken like the girl's in the car, and the mask of laughter that was her friend's worn by the soldiers brandishing their guns.

Grayson knows what he must do: now that he's aware, he must accept. He keeps breathing, ever more slowly, and after a while the tears come and he knows he's managed, as he has a hundred times before.

For several days Grayson doesn't show up at the café. At first Ros wonders if he's changed his routine or if she said something wrong. Later she worries that something has happened to him.

When she finally sees him, limping along in his ski outfit, he's outside on the sidewalk talking to a woman. He smiles and waves when he notices her staring through the window.

"You look like an ad from an athletic magazine," she says

cheerfully when Grayson walks through the door.

"I'm too old to show up in ads. And my leg wouldn't go down too well."

"Wrong, my friend. Advanced middle age is their target market. And physical impediments evoke sympathy."

"You're full of compliments, Ros. How could I have accused you of being a grouch?"

"How could you?"

Grayson puts down his hat and gloves and walks to the counter to place his order. When he returns to the table Ros is staring out the window, watching snow turning to mush. Each passing car pushes brown spray from under its wheels onto the sidewalk. Bits of it fly at the window and turn into dirty streaks.

Ros asks why he's going skiing on a day like this. "The light's a bit flat, don't you think?"

"It didn't look bad when I left the house. But maybe I'll change my plans. Stick around here, for a while." Then, glancing around the café, he says, "Ros, can we talk?"

"We *are* talking."

Grayson beams. "Listen to this—you'll like it. You've got yourself an apartment."

Ros' features freeze, her eyes staring at the coffee mug in Grayson's hand. Then, as if talking to herself, she asks, "Did you really say that just now?" A moment later her expression turns exuberant, but not for long, as disbelief once more enters her thoughts. "Are you serious?"

"Bigger too, and the same rent," she hears Grayson say.

"Come on. How did you swing that?"

"I talked to Les Bernstein. He likes you."

"Bernstein, huh?" She thinks of the short man everyone in

town seems to know and respect. He's not one of her regulars, but she's talked to him at numerous gallery openings.

"He also wants to talk to you about a restaurant he's building down valley. He may need art for his walls."

"You think he'd buy some?"

"That, or he'll let you exhibit."

"You mean I may be able to use photography to pay for part of my rent?" Ros' eyes are back on the grey outside as she sighs, "I don't know how you did it, Grayson." Then she adds more cheerfully, "but it earns you at least one free cappuccino."

She quivers a bit, turns toward him and reaches for his shoulders as if to hug him and says, "I feel like going out there and dancing in the street." Her voice is expressive now, but her face is still severe. Grayson can tell she's holding back tears.

"Don't do that, Ros. You'll break a leg in that slush."

HIS HEART IS POUNDING AND his bad leg is on fire as he runs up Smuggler Mountain. But he feels strong, knowing he's making good time. Another half a mile or so and he can stop.

A dog barks somewhere above him, then he hears a voice. His breathing drowns out most of the sound, but as he comes around the next switch he sees a woman. Tall, wearing a parka. Above her, coming straight down the mountainside and ignoring the path, is her dog, a Jack Russell Terrier. Grayson nods to the woman as he passes and then he's alone again. Two more switches and he'll hit the snow. He'll come in at less than 25 minutes, for sure. Maybe he'll clock a new record.

Then he sees the chipmunk, almost runs over it. A miserable bit of fluff, brown against the mud-colored trail, lying on its back and shuddering miserably. "That fucking dog," Grayson hears himself swear.

He crouches down to turn the creature on its legs and as his hand approaches, the convulsing body energizes itself, tremors turning to agonizing twitches as it tries to get back whatever it takes to escape. Grayson hesitates, afraid he'll get scratched or bitten, but all the chipmunk is capable of is more twitching. Only one of its hind legs participates. The other, its ligaments torn or bones crushed, hangs idly at an impossible angle. Then Grayson sees the crimson line, thin as if drawn by an accountant's pencil, starting at the corner of the creature's mouth and disappearing under its neck.

He gets up, stumbles around nervously, feeling queasy and wondering what to do, and that's when he sees the rock above him, red against the washed out background and sitting on the soil loosely. He struggles up between tufts of grass beaten down by winter and slippery from melting snow.

Grayson carries the boulder back and lifts it high. In his incensed mind it's not the wounded chipmunk that will be released from agony, but the killer dog whose sin against nature must be righted. He slams the rock down.

When he rolls it aside he's grateful there isn't a lot of blood. Still, he tries to look away as he picks up the dead animal by its tail and hurls it toward a stand of scrub oaks. His arm is still stretched out, a darkish streak against a sky of fair-weather cumulus, when he notices the bits of fur that have stuck to his fingers. Grayson feels a surge of nausea and tries to ignore it. Instinctively, he starts moving away and breaks into a run.

Further uphill he comes to a large patch of snow and that's where he stops. He bends down and rubs his palms against the gritty surface, first averting his eyes but seconds later fastidiously examining his fingers. There are no fur bits left, but what he does find is a bright smudge of blood along his index. Images of the cocky terrier and the pathetic chipmunk, its meager chest heaving and its surviving limbs pawing at nothingness, explode in his mind and his anger swells. The knots that have formed in his stomach grow into fists. Grayson closes his lids for a moment and when he allows himself to reopen them, he notices the jerks.

Small spasms swift as lightning, blurry in front of his stunned eyes—two seemingly independent hands taking orders from who knows where. Then his elbows and shoulders join in, possessed by energy that becomes ever more disobedient. He watches his hands flail and flap disjointedly now, gesticulating without imparting a message, waving to bystanders that don't exist, intent on striking anything in their illogical path. Occasionally they hit each other.

His fear grows; he dreads what is to come. Grayson summons what trickle of strength he has left, attempts to concentrate, tries to recall what to do, and comes up with this: he has to breathe. Fill his lungs to capacity, then exhale. In deeply—out slowly, in deeply—out slowly, so goes the recording that plays in his mind. And in time the spasms in his shoulders abate, the pistons in his elbows lose their power and the blurs that are his hands turns into solid, static matter, as if someone had yanked their batteries.

Grayson looks at them as tough they'd just been given to him: spidery veins crawling from under his sleeve and losing themselves between his knuckles, healthy nails bordered by cuticles cracked by the dry mountain air. And no cuts, no major bruises. No bandaged hands this time. He's thankful.

When he gets up he realizes how exhausted he is. His limbs feel leaden and his mind is flooded with fog so dense he finds it painful to keep his eyes open. And yet, as he stands resting, he can't help taking in the splendid expanse below him. Grayson's gaze rests on the east end for a while, then dwells on the silver thread that leaves Aspen toward Independence Pass, before moving back to the town centre and finally settling on a large stucco house far below him. The walls are ochre, a shade lighter than the color of New Mexico's adobe houses. From where Grayson stands, the most conspicuous feature are the skylights. It would be impossible to count them now, with the dazzle of the morning sun uniting them into one pulsating field of light. But Grayson doesn't have to count them. He knows there are sixteen. He planned it this way.

There was a time when he was proud of his house. Seventy-four hundred square feet on a knoll overlooking Aspen! But recently he's been uncomfortable about owning it. He and Samantha have argued—he convinced they could live in something a quarter the size, she wanting to build an addition for a gym. He listens in on their argument, hears words designed to sting, the syllables amplified by his brain and echoing somewhere in the dome of his skull.

And then the smell. Gasoline-laden air enveloping him, constricting his lungs and making measured breathing impossible. He knows from experience that frustration or disappointment are now impossible. Emotions require energy. All Grayson can do is resign himself, use the five or ten seconds he has to sit or lie down, find a position where he won't get hurt. But as he starts turning his head, he has a thought—that if he keeps looking at his mansion, glues his eyes to it, maybe he can avert what's coming. And in a way it works.

The smell stays. It makes his head giddy and his breath surges and falls in short swells because he doesn't want to breathe, couldn't breathe the nauseating fumes. But something else begins to happen, something that takes his attention elsewhere. His mansion starts to melt.

First its outlines blur, then it contracts like in some bizarre footage from Honey-I-Shrank-The-Kids. The ground floor disappears, then the upstairs starts to dissolve. For a few moments the roof sticks out of the light-brown liquid that's seeping into his knoll, then that is gone too.

I'm going insane, Grayson thinks while bending down. He grabs at the snow with both hands and feels its texture, the fact that he did the same just minutes ago completely forgotten. His brain informs him that yesterday's sun must have turned the snow heavy and the night frozen it. He can tell that makes sense; that's why it feels so coarse and granular.

He brings his palms to his face and pushes the crystals against his forehead and cheeks, grinds them into the sides of his nose and up his temples. It all feels harsh, gravel-like, but it numbs his skin and his senses and that is welcome. When Grayson lets go, he sees bits of washed-out red on the snow that's left in his hands. This is real, he tells himself. What I see is my blood and that is fucking real!

He forces himself to look downhill. His house is gone but his neighbour's, which has been built after his, still stands. And so do the cottonwoods and aspens he's planted behind and to the sides of the house. He covers his eyes, pressing the icy tips of his thumbs into his eye sockets, and unleashes a kaleidoscope of throbbing purple, yellow and black. Then he summons the courage to look again, through the prison-window bars of his fingers this time, and he sees that nothing has changed.

His thoughts race aimlessly through the swirling mists of his brain, eager to find a connection, a fragment of truth, a single shard of hope. Yet he also understands that the place he's in knows no absolutes, only endless contradictions whose components change even as they are observed. For every aspiration there is inertia, equal in weight and simultaneous. Hope is met with despair in the twilight of his two minds; dreams and night-mares coexist. Grayson's one mind vaguely remembers a world of truths somewhere, while the other is trapped in the agony of his imagined gasoline swirls and his evaporated house. Being here is not a solution, he can see that, but even so, he doesn't resist. At least it gives him a space to rest. An oasis of sorts—the sanctuary of opposing realities.

A second, a minute of refuge, then the minds engage again. Get up and breathe and go home, demands one, and Grayson briefly appreciates the sanity of this argument, but then he recognizes its lack of logic. How can I breathe the unbreathable, and what home is there to go to, anyway? And he can see the sense in this too.

But eventually he does get up and breathe and that's when he starts wondering if he still exists. If someone came around the corner, would they see him? Or is he gone like the house and this is where it all ends?

Dead on a positive note. Being able to help Ros. Making good time on his jog, despite his fucked-up leg and the dying chipmunk. *On a positive note.* He likes this idea and his mind keeps repeating it frantically, and as it does so the last traces of the gasoline smell leave and Grayson becomes aware of his throbbing leg and sees that his pants are torn on one knee and that the snow below him is soiled with crimson streaks.

He turns to look in the direction where his house was and where it should be again. The morning sun, still reflecting off the skylights, blinds him for a second or two. But when his sight returns he sees two things: a couple of switches below a woman hiking up toward him, and in the distance his house.

He cries, not knowing whether from relief that he's come back once more or from the hundredweight of pain that's settled on his soul. He tastes the brittle winter air, cautiously at first and then in big gulps.

Grayson is on the white ash floor in his bedroom, meditating as he always does after things spin out of control. He's been at it for nearly an hour and now, with his eyes closed, he imagines himself levitating. He's in the horizontal, about four feet above the ground, his mind's eye taking in the opening to the bathroom. The sinks are at the same level as his body, the rim of the oversized tub slightly below. He's weightless but one thing separates him from perfection: he can't turn smoothly. His feet are slowly shifting to the right, toward the wall with the Miró etchings on it, but the movement is jolty, as if someone made him turn by moving a sticky knob on a radio dial. It's taken him years to achieve seamlessness. This is a step backward.

Grayson abandons the exercise. Sitting up he reflects on his near collision and this morning's jog. Two episodes within one week! Something that hasn't happened for a long time and he can't even guess at the cause. And then recognizing the woman coming toward him as Ros—and running away from her. The worst thing he could have done.

Grayson suppresses his thoughts and allows himself to slide onto his back, determined to drift back into a state of escape. His meditation rug feels soft and warm under him. He decides to go back to a breathing exercise. Never mind levitating. The simpler, the better.

He concentrates on his breath, draws out its rhythm, lengthens it until it leaves the realm of time and joins the pulse of eternity. He imagines it entering through his forehead, bright-blue energy, radiant like the petal of a cornflower in July or the wing of a tropical bird. Then he lets it flow down his torso, through his abdomen and down his legs, before it leaves through the tips of his toes. When inhaling he feels his forehead extend inwards until it almost touches the back of his skull. As the breath moves down through his body he feels its healing touch, warm and tingling.

Grayson has left his mind behind.

IT'S EVENING AND THE SKY is shedding bloated, pure-white flakes. Gusts of mountain air send them soaring and tumbling in patterns so bold you'd think they were weightless. But each flake is destined to land, to collide with the furrowed surface of an old fence or a withered blade of grass or the black harshness of asphalt, and when it does so its clumsiness is exposed. Tree branches strain as newcomers merge into the canopy of flakes already settled. Some of the older and more exposed limbs will break off long before morning, snapping with the sound of a pistol muffled by the clamour of the storm.

Inside Grayson's house the windows to the west would be impossible to see through, if not the same wind that carried the snow to them also blew bits of it away. Jack looks out at the figure struggling up his driveway: a pair of boots fighting their way toward him, leaving knee-deep tracks. Above the snow a couple of inches of leg and then a puffy parka, zippered up high. Only a fragment of face shows; the rest is shielded by a thick scarf and woollen hat. It could be man or woman, this figure, but Grayson doesn't have to guess. He's dreaded this moment and he wonders how Ros will deal with him.

He stiffly opens the door. A long moment passes as Ros unzips, unlaces and finally takes off hat and scarf. When she's finished, the snow on the tiled hallway floor has already disintegrated into puddles.

Neither of them has yet spoken when Ros walks by Grayson, looks up at the high ceilings and the vastness of the living room that opens before them and says, "I can't believe how big this place is. Like a dozen of my apartments."

Grayson didn't expect that. She's acting as if nothing had happened. He cautiously says, "A bit ostentatious, don't you think?"

"Come on, everything in this valley is," Ros answers. She takes in the openness of the space and the simplicity with which it's decorated. "I think it's great."

Grayson steps up to the kitchen island and asks what she wants to drink. "I can make you a Margarita. Or you can have some wine, if you prefer."

"Wine. And then let's cut the crap. You know why I'm here." Here it is. Her eyes are ablaze.

"Ros, I know I owe you an…"

"I'm not looking for an apology. I want to know what happened, up there on the mountain this morning. You come at me looking like you've been through a meat grinder, face ripped up and pants torn, and you treat me as if we'd once met at someone else's dinner party."

"Ros, I'm sorry."

"That doesn't cut it, you know that. I want to understand. The other day you told me we were friends—what was that all about?"

Grayson is nervous and afraid. He busies himself with corkscrew and wine bottle. "Christ, we are! We are friends, Ros."

"That's not the impression I got this morning."

"It's a long story that starts many years ago. And it's very personal." He wants to seek out her eyes and plead, but instead he looks at the bottle and her empty glass.

"And?" Ros prods, testily.

"And this is a small town."

"A few days ago, you told me we should help each other because we lived in the same small town."

Grayson buys himself time. He pours her wine, then opens the fridge and gets himself a can of Diet Coke. Finally, he looks up at Ros. "I do want to tell you. But we need ground rules."

"What for?"

"I need to talk about something very personal."

"You already said that, Grayson."

"Well, I'd like it to stay between us. I trust you."

Ros throws up her arms. "If you trust me there's no bloody need for rules," she says sharply.

They're still standing in the kitchen, except she now has her hand on his arm. "I had no idea," Ros says. "And here I was concerned about my cracked crown."

"And your apartment."

"Big deal."

"Your problems are a big deal, Ros. It's just that mine are taking place in a different realm. My brain."

"I wasn't talking about the thing with the disappearing house."

"Oh."

"No, the whole baggage. Getting shot, being paralyzed, losing your family. That's real enough, Grayson! And you never mentioned a thing."

"It's not something I want to advertise."

"I understand." She tries to make eye contact, but Grayson is staring at the granite surface of the counter. He keeps pushing around a stack of napkins and two candlesticks, rearranging them endlessly. "You know, I've always wondered how people can cope with that kind of thing. How do you find the strength to come back? It must take a lot of courage." She reaches to cup his hand and gives it a squeeze.

"Not courage." His eyes are still on the counter.

Ros looks for something to say. "But you did come back, didn't you?" she tries.

"Eventually, yes."

"Eventually?"

Grayson raises his eyes. "Ros, I don't think I can deal with any more of this tonight. Why don't I drive you home? Or you can sleep here, if you want."

"Right. Your wife comes back from the spa and the neighbors tell her they saw me leave here in the morning." Ros is pleased she's found a way to lighten the conversation. "Imagine, me. The cappuccino lady."

Grayson wonders how Samantha would react. He says, "If she felt threatened, it would be because you're an artist. But anyway, she won't be back till next week. Journeying to a spa is not worth it if you go for a day or two."

"She's growing on me, Grayson. But yes, drive me home."

Grayson is tossing restlessly. His sheets are clammy as they often are when he dreams. He watches the stainless-steel doors shut. He knows it's supposed to mean closure, but it never is. It's the beginning.

He watches himself in the spotless mirror, then notices his shoes reflect light. When he looks up again the Fedex driver is there. That puzzles him because the elevator hasn't stopped. Grayson wants to see his face or at least see him in profile. But as always, the Fedex man has his back to him. All he gets to see is his dark-blue, purple-trimmed uniform and above that a bronzed neck contrasting with silvery hair. He studies that bit of neck with its enigmatic tattoo fragment: part of an anchor or a whale fin?

Grayson lowers his eyes and sees the well-kept hand holding an envelope. He asks himself how such a man has become a Fedex driver—that's how the dream always goes. First generation immigrant, he remembers, with a Maltese degree in economics. This conclusion makes him feel awful. Grayson sees himself kneeling on his meditation rug, tapping his forehead on the ground, berating himself for his arrogance.

Then the parking lot attendant steps out of his booth. He's smiling, trying to be agreeable, eager to be on Jack's good side. "The keys are inside, Mr. Grayson." He's said that same sentence for a decade, ever since Grayson has parked there. Grayson watches himself bend down again, hears his whispered pleas for forgiveness. He's never even asked the man where he lived, whether he had a family.

Driving along King Street helps his mind wander. The fleeting images of office towers on the polished hood of his car remind him where he belongs. The nation's power centers, that's what these buildings are. And he, Grayson, one of the chosen few. He's managed to create a life in the Sweet Spot and, better yet, Marlene and the boys can be part of it too.

But dwelling on these thoughts becomes disturbing to him,

and once more he becomes aware of his conceit. And when the light below his speedometer starts flashing orange, he knows things will go terribly wrong. Everything is speeding up: the 24-hour sign at the gas station, unlocking the tank flap, the hum of the pump and the racing digital numbers—all a furious blur now. The sickening smell is there and to the side of the building is the black van with the bluish exhaust coming from underneath.

And then time is suspended and things become simple. The two men stepping from the pay booth crowd out all other awareness. He fixes his eyes on the blond one, the one with the cropped light hair, and watches him reach into his jacket. Grayson knows this is where he's supposed to do something to avert what's coming, but he'll end up just standing there.

He moans, gripping his sweat-soaked sheets. When he sees the flash of the exploding gun his thigh is already on fire.

JACK GRAYSON AVOIDS TELEVISION; HE stopped his subscription a couple of years ago. Yet, here in the café as in most public places, the persistent drone of news is inescapable. After scanning the nearby tables, at this hour mostly occupied by locals, his eyes come to rest on the wall-mounted, oversized screen just as the image focuses on the Secretary of State's gloating visage. "We came, we saw, he died," she exclaims, then laughs heartily. The interviewer appears amused too.

Libya again, Grayson realizes. He recalls reading up on the carnage in Tripoli a few days ago. He found it hard to concentrate on the words then, his eyes darting back to the image of the old man whose face was hidden behind a pair of hands so worn and cracked they could have been Libya's sun-baked, bomb-torn earth itself. Underneath was a pair of parched lips that must have tasted the salt of too many tears, and below that a weathered chin covered with white bristles. The background was made up of bits of torn buildings and twisted car parts and garbage, an irrelevant collage save for one object: a piece of arm that would have blended into the rubble were it not for the bloodied shirt sleeve around it.

Grayson had studied it, feeling the blaze of his anger rise. He'd wanted to push the paper away, move on to something more pleasant or at least trivial, but he found he couldn't. His eyes had moved back to the old man's shielded face instead and tried to define its grip on him. For a second Grayson had believed he could see dignity shine through this wretchedness. But then he'd dismissed that thought. Not dignity. Resignation, acceptance.

He turns back to the TV screen. "I must never trust those fuckers again, Republicans or Democrats", he says to himself. All of them peddling the same fantasy: emasculating a brutal dictator, taking away his horror weapons, democratizing a nation. He should have known. By the time you arrive on the tenth floor of the political edifice you're so compromised you're scum, no matter what ideals you once held. And when you get to the penthouse suite you become the devil itself.

Grayson hears the voice of his father, droning on about the nobility of war.

His eyes settle on Ros who's weaving her way through the café, carrying his cappuccino. He's been wondering about her. Now that he's told her, is she going to pretend nothing happened or will she want to know more? He doesn't know about himself, either. Would he be prepared to talk more if she asked?

He puts on his best face. "How are you doing, kid?"

"A bit frustrated, actually." When she sees the change in his expression, she adds, "Nothing to do with you, Grayson. Just a small crisis with my art. A decision I have to make."

"I see."

"Someone has asked me to do a commission. Good money, too."

"And what's there to be frustrated about?"

"I've never done one, that's all. I'm not sure I want the pressure and I don't like the guy. And then there's what he wants it for."

"What's that?"

"He's getting this painting done. A knock-off of a classic that shows Napoleon and his entourage going into battle. He wants to hang it over the fireplace in his new ranch."

"Ah, Bonaparte visits Colorado. And I imagine your prospective client gets to be Napoleon?"

"No, that wouldn't work. He wants people to classify this as a masterpiece, so Napoleon has to look himself."

"I get it."

"The general riding up front with Bonaparte, he's the one that would wear my client's face. And his sons and sons-in-law make up the rest of the officer corps. There'll be six of them, including the big guy."

"And what exactly would your role be?"

"I'm supposed to capture the right angles and facial expressions, so the painter he's hired can copy them."

Grayson sips his cappuccino, considering. "How about saying no?"

"He's offered me nine grand, Grayson! One for each of the five lesser characters and four for himself—that's how he said it. Even that part had to be offensive."

"It's a lot of money."

"For two or three days' work? Beats the pittance I make here."

"Come on, Ros. These five-dollar latte productions must pay off."

"It's a franchise. The supplies are expensive. Plus, consider Aspen rents, Grayson. Also don't forget most other operators have a year-round season. I get seven good months and the rest is a loss."

"I guess you have to take it then, this commission?"

"No, I can afford to turn him down, thanks to your introduction to Les Bernstein. The only reason I'm tempted is that I'd get out of this tight spot."

Grayson means to tell Ros not to sell her soul, but someone calls her away. And when he returns for another cappuccino in the afternoon he forgets, because Ros gets back to the big topic.

"About the other night. I sense you told me more than you wanted to, Grayson. Don't worry about it."

"That's not it. I just had to quit because I need to do it in small doses."

"It's painful for you to talk about it."

"Yes, but I thought about it most of the day. There's more."

Ros wonders how much more. They sit for a while, staring at the distance. Then she says, "Your wife is still away, I take it?"

"Three more days."

"Will she look after you?"

"I'll be all right, yes."

"That's not what I'm asking." Ros is searching for the right words. "You've been through a lot the last few days. You say you need someone to talk to."

"You mean do I talk to my wife?"

"That's what I mean."

"It's complicated. We both had to deal with a lot of pain. Before we met."

"So what are you saying?"

"Sorry?"

"Well, will you tell her what happened while she was away?"

Seconds go by as Grayson thinks, unaware that his hand squeezes the empty cardboard cup into a sausage. "I will tell her I had episodes. I may not tell her we talked."

Ros considers. "Why don't you come to my place for dinner tomorrow?" she says. "That way I'll get to have my ground rules, too."

"Which are?"

"One is, I'm a lousy cook but you can't bitch. The other, you can't drink Diet Coke."

Dinner is unremarkable: macaroni with cheese and ground beef mixed in. But Grayson has brought two bottles of Australian Shiraz, one of which stands empty, its dense green glass distorting the flicker of a lone candle.

So far they've stayed with safe topics. The number of tourists in town, the mediocre snow conditions, the physics lectures Ros attends, and Grayson's new interest in plants. In the background a Miles Davis track plays. Grayson has asked Ros to write down the title.

All evening long they've both known what they'll end up talking about. But Grayson needs to be sure that Ros really wants to listen and Ros has been waiting for the right opportunity. Now she knows it's here.

"Come on, Grayson, off to the kitchen sink," she orders. "The most meaningful conversations take place while doing dishes."

"You're saying that to break the ice. No more talk about the weather and our small town?"

"I thought we'd broken the ice a few days ago. But seriously, the only decent talks I ever had with my mother or grandmother were in the kitchen."

"I guess men don't do dishes down under."

"Men have better things to do."

"I have visions of them sitting behind the house shooting at flocks of passing kangaroos," Grayson says.

"Some do, unfortunately. But flock is strictly incorrect. It's called a mob."

"A mob, then."

"Tell me about the men in your family, Grayson."

"My grandfather died when I was little. I adored him."

Ros watches the smile on his face. "No adoration for your father, though?"

"Why do you say that?" Grayson is amazed how effortlessly she's zoomed in.

"The dream you told me about. Where your mother beckoned you in. You said she didn't hug or kiss you. Just turned around and started walking up the stairs where your father was."

"I'm not sure that one was a dream."

"Call it a near-death experience then. Real enough, isn't it?" Ros reminds herself to be gentle. "Tell me about your Dad," she says softly. "I'll wash and you dry."

"It's a painful topic."

"I understand."

Grayson reflects. He doesn't know where to start or whether he wants to start. Images of Marlene, their new receptionist, flit through his mind. And then his father crowds in, a bigger presence than he was in life even, his arrogant face etched into Grayson's brain with a torch. Distant, vindictive, capable of inflicting pain that will throb forever. "No, you don't understand, Ros."

"Why don't we start where we ended the other night?"

"Waking up in the hospital."

"Yes, and your wife bent over you."

"Right. And no pain."

Ros puts down her towel, moves a bit closer. "No pain is bad, isn't it?"

"For a moment I thought it was great. Then I tried to sit up. I pushed my hands down and that worked, but when I tried to help along with my feet there was nothing. No hurt, no sensation. I couldn't tell whether I still had legs and feet, but Marlene's face said she knew."

Beads of sweat form on Grayson's forehead. He half expects the smell to come, the way it always does. Almost imperceptible at first, as if a gasoline-soaked rag had been left lying twenty feet away. Then fumes all around him, wanting to fill his lungs, to force out the good air he needed to keep living.

Standing with Ros now he concentrates on his breathing and his nostrils welcome the moisture-laden air that rises from the kitchen sink. It helps. He inhales the lavender detergent scent.

Ros watches intently as he takes one of the glasses she's just dried, fills it with water and drinks. Then another series of deliberate, long breaths and his explanation. "Breathing helps me fend off my episodes. At least sometimes."

"God, Grayson. We don't need to do this. You know we can talk about it another time." She hasn't even thought of his talking bringing on a seizure.

He weighs her comment, tells her that he's wondered whether digging up all the old stuff will only worsen his condition. But he's convinced himself it's the solution, not the problem. "Convinced is the wrong word, actually. Decided. I've decided it's the answer."

And then he continues, explaining how Marlene said he may

not be able to use his lower body for a while and how he was too afraid to ask how long a while was or what she'd been told.

"The next day the boys came to see me. It was painful. We'd started playing tennis together. And ski. No more of that."

She looks at him, trying to imagine. "How could you cope?"

"That's what I like about you, Ros. The look on your face right now. Pure sincerity."

Ros holds his stare. She wonders if she should feel uncomfortable, but instead she only feels his pain.

"How could I cope? I coped because there was a system designed to make me. Nurses flitting by, reminding me that I had to eat. The surgeon checking in. Aides who washed my armpits and wiped my ass. Later dieticians and radiologists. All that."

Ros ignores the trail of bitterness that's oozing through his voice. "No rest, I suppose?" It's all she can think of saying.

"I went to fill up my tank and next thing I got shot in the spine and I was a cripple."

She says, "No longer, you aren't."

Grayson wipes cutlery, taking more time than necessary. He looks shaken up. After a while, he holds up a fork and announces, "Last one."

They move back to the dining room table, careful not to trip over the bins and boxes that cover much of the small apartment. Once they sit, Ros steers the conversation to her new apartment and how it will change her life.

Before long, Grayson finds himself opening the second bottle of wine. He hasn't drunk for years and now he knows why. It feels good.

Ros' couch is comfortable but Grayson finds it hard to fall asleep. His mind is on Marlene asking for a divorce. If he explained it to Ros, she'd say, "I don't blame her", and he'd answer, "I didn't either. In a way, I was relieved." And Ros would be stunned. He wonders whether he'll ever find the courage to tell her about Marlene. She'll think I'm a monster. And probably I am.

When sleep finally grips him, it comes with a forceful dream. As it grips his mind Grayson instantly understands he's hemmed in, his movements limited to a few steps in each direction. And what's worse is that he can't figure out why. There is no cage, no barbed wire. And there are no walls. His view is unobstructed. He can see the needle that is the CN Tower in the haze and beyond that a fragment of gun-metal blue lake. He's in Toronto and he even knows where: he's standing inside his living room waiting for Marlene and the boys to get home. He paces up and down, noticing that all his possessions are gone. It's as if he didn't exist any longer.

Marlene and the boys, where are they? Grayson surprises himself by not caring whether they'll ever come back. They've known him at his best and now they're between him and…what?

Grayson knows. He doesn't want to give it a name but he feels it well up in him, tightening his chest, wanting all of him for itself and ready to lash out at anyone near him. He shrinks, hoping even more intensely that Marlene and the boys won't come home, because he knows they'll end up suffering his abuse. If he's to come out of this he has to be alone with his fear. He understands that. He must learn to accept his limitations. Confront the monster within him.

"Well, did you confront your demons?" The voice is strangely distorted and comes from a distance, but Grayson knows it belongs to Ros. He paces forward, looking for her and this time he's free to go as far as he wants to.

The street he follows is deserted and the haze feels wet on his skin. In the distance he sees an imposing brick building with steps leading up to a set of magnificent doors and a sandstone arch over them. He looks at the chiselled inscription and it occurs to him that he's meant to memorize it. But no sooner does he start to read that a uniformed guard asks him to enter and go upstairs to the main hall.

"Did you confront your demons?" he hears Ros again, this time a lot clearer. Aware of the need to hurry Grayson starts to run down a long hallway, passing countless doors. The further he goes, the cooler the air gets. The sweat on his brow dries but it still feels sticky.

Near the end of the corridor, he hears the voice a third time and then he sees the assembled crowd and up on a platform Ros. She wears a purple robe and has the head of a lioness. On the wall behind her is large golden symbol: a circle within a circle. He can tell he's in a courtroom.

"The demons!" Ros prompts him sternly, letting him know this is more than just a question. He's being interrogated.

"At first, I thought I'd get Marlene and the boys back," Grayson answers sheepishly. "I'd overcome my dark side. Heal myself and return a new man, worthy of them."

"And?" Ros' brows are getting thicker and Grayson is confused, not sure lionesses are supposed to have eyebrows. A deep crease starts forming on Ros' forehead and he panics. Christ, she's my judge, he thinks, but then he realizes he probably told Ros everything because he wanted to be judged.

"And?"

He can't bear her gaze. "I went into free fall instead," he mumbles. He's on a witness stand, his eyes trained on the railing in front of him, studying the rich patina of the wood, the hundreds of tightly arranged wormholes. This was a fruit tree once, he thinks, puzzled that he should know that.

"You mean it got worse?" Ros' voice thunders.

"The man I hoped to find wasn't there. I was so consumed with anger, there was nothing else left."

"There was no You?"

"Either that or all of me had turned into anger. I spent half the day at rehab and the other half tearing up the world. No progress on the medical front whatsoever."

"Then how do you explain that you are standing before me now, a fully restored man?"

Fully restored? Grayson wonders how she can say that. He gets confused as to where in time this interrogation is taking place. He decides to ignore her question. "Two years after I left Marlene, I finally got the right therapist."

"How did that happen?" Ros is now hitting keys on a machine in front of her, recording her questions and Grayson's answers.

He notices her hands: they aren't those of a lioness. The long slender fingers and rounded nails unmistakably belong to Ros. "I found Hendrick," he shrugs.

"And what did he do?"

"He put me back on my path."

"Ah, your path," Ros says pensively, her beautiful hands now relaxing and her feline facial features morphing back into human form. "Following the path is all that matters."

Ros gets up and Grayson is incredibly relieved. He feels he has no care and knows his suffering is at an end. As if from a great distance he hears Ros thank those present and watches her prepare to leave the room. Before she steps through the backdoor she turns back and looks straight at Grayson and repeats. "The path is what matters!"

GRAYSON SEES THE TAXI CRAWL down the driveway and goes to the door. By the time he gets there, Samantha is already coming up the staircase.

"Hello Jack, darling," she says, kissing him on the cheek and rushing by him. He stands there, watching the driver struggle with the two suitcases.

"That's thirty-four dollars, sir," he says.

Grayson is amazed. Evidently, the driver knows that Samantha won't come back out. He hesitates, before asking: "What makes you know that I'm the one who pays?"

"I'm sorry, sir. I assumed…"

"No, no. You assumed correctly. I'm just curious how you knew."

The driver looks uncomfortable. "I just didn't think, that's all."

"I bet your instinct told you."

The driver considers, then grins. "Is the lady your wife?"

"Yes, she's my wife," Grayson replies.

"She's just…she's the type, you know. Very beautiful, but high maintenance. She's used to others taking care of things." He looks at Grayson curiously, not sure whether his words will meet with approval or resentment.

Grayson laughs and pays. He adds a good tip.

Samantha is coming down the corridor. She's wearing black knee-high boots, a black jumpsuit with a conspicuous zipper running down its front and a vibrant turquoise green silk scarf. Her hair and makeup are perfect, as always. Her perfume hits Jack's nostrils as she passes. Always on the run, Samantha.

She disappears but the clicking of her heels tells him she's heading for the bathroom. Then he hears the water run. When he gets there she is standing at the marble sink brushing her teeth. Her boots now lie on the floor, as does her scarf. Grayson sits down on the rim of the bathtub and watches her rinse.

"How was the spa?" he asks when she's finished.

"Exquisite, as always. You should really try it, Jack." She looks at him intently. "Come along just once. It would be so good for you."

"What did you do?"

"Oh, apart from the usual stuff?"

Grayson, who's only been to a spa once and hated it, assumes her reference to the usual covers beautification and dieting—or is it cleansing? "Yes, apart from that."

"Scrubs, my dear, out-of-this-world scrubs." She walks out of the bathroom as if the conversation were over.

Grayson remains sitting, shouting, "What kind of scrubs?" after her.

"The first day I tried a conditioning scrub. Oatmeal and jojoba, with beta-carotene mixed in. Makes your skin glow." He can tell from her voice that she's right around the corner in the walk-in closet.

"I thought beta-carotene made you red. No?"

"Don't be silly, Jack. Why do you always have to ridicule my interests?" Now she stands at the bathroom door in her bra, looking at him accusingly.

Grayson gets up. "No, I'm interested. What other rubs?"

"Scrubs, Jack. There was a thing called the Razuli Ritual. You should have seen the place they had that in. All Persian mosaic, with a huge cupola overhead and shafts of sunlight cutting through the steam. Louise and I loved it."

"Louise Bernstein was there?"

"Yeah! Apparently she visits once every two months. Oh, by the way Jack, Louise told me about this seer." She walks up to him, holds him around his waist. "Don't say no now, darling. We have to make an appointment."

"What, to see the seer?" Grayson asks dryly.

"I knew it. You have to make fun of everything," she playfully pounds her fists on his chest.

"Why would I go to a seer, Samantha? Just because Louise Bernstein likes her?"

"It's a he, to start with. And apparently he doesn't take new clients. If we get in it's only because of Louise."

"I can see you want to go, but personally I'm hoping that the divine Louise will fail."

Samantha turns away again, disappearing around the corner. "You're hopeless," he hears her continue, "but this is one thing I want you to do with me, Jack." Then she's back, looking at him imploringly. "This is very important to me. I'd really like you to come."

"Okay, if you feel that way I'll think about it."

Samantha is headed for the walk-in closet again and Grayson follows her. "We don't have to fly anywhere, do we?"

"No, darling. He's in Boulder."

"Oh, Christ, Samantha—that's still a whole day!"

She walks up to him, snuggling against him. "Let's make two days out of it, Jack. We'll stay at that heavenly hotel overnight. What's its name again? Oh Jack, you've noticed, haven't you?" She looks up at him expectantly.

"Noticed what, Samantha?" Grayson answers sheepishly. He knows her question implies that something meaningful has changed, but he can't figure it out.

"Your hairstyle?" he probes, surveying the amber waves below his eyes.

"My hairstyle?" she protests in disbelief. "My hair color, you idiot!"

ROS IS BATHED IN AGREEABLE warmth; she loves the skylights above her living room. She's only lived here two days and already she knows that she'll never want to be in a dark place again. A few feet from where she stands is the sliding glass door that leads to a small deck facing the mountain. More light!

The boxes that cluttered her old apartment are stacked up where her new living room will be, but Ros is in no hurry to unpack. Right now, she's enjoying her morning cup of Columbian in her new surroundings.

Her deal with Les Bernstein is a good one. The restaurant he owns has two sections, one of which will feature her art. If any of it sells, her landlord takes twenty-five percent and applies the rest against rent. Twenty-five percent is half of what her gallery would take. What more could she want?

Ros wonders if she can do as much for Grayson as he's done for her. He seems desperate to talk, yet when he gets there he often pulls back. Like someone at the rim of a smouldering crater shrinking back from the surging heat. And sometimes she's the one who wants to withdraw, exhausted by the intensity of his words and eager to resort to an easier topic. Ironically, that's usually when Grayson persists. Two needles trying to play the same piece of vinyl. They've got to get into the same groove to make it work.

Ros realizes that logic won't help when listening to Grayson. Not when she's dealing with the swell of his emotions. But she's got a grip on it: she knows what's at its center. It's something to do with his father. And she relates to that.

Ros thinks of the small clapboard house in the outback, half a day's train ride from Darwin, and her father's pride in it. He was a good man. Stern and without imagination, but decent, his universe the nearby dairy where he worked, the house and his family. Once, when she spent some saved-up money on a sketch-book and colored pencils her dad took them back, telling her that drawing was not for their kind of people. Helping Mother and saving for a dowry would bring her stability and happiness.

She hears him talk. His speech is agonizingly slow and he frequently stops to let a word or an expression hang in the air. He calls her Rosalyn. Decades have passed and she lives on the other side of the world now, but as she listens to her memories she feels like the girl she once was. Rosalyn.

Then she remembers the phone call she got and hears her mother's voice, nearly breaking under the weight of anguish, but her message oddly condensed so that she can keep the call under three minutes. "I must go now, dear. Long distance."

How helpless Ros had felt that night, trying to figure out who her father had been. She knew he'd never said an unkind word to her, but then they'd never talked. And now that he was dead she'd never get to know him. The finality of that devastated her.

She had turned to Grayson that evening, just one of her café regulars sipping a cappuccino, but one who unexpectedly understood her need. He sensed she didn't want to talk much and so he just sat with her until she closed up, then drove her back to her apartment. He offered to come in and make her hot chocolate, so she wouldn't be all alone. Ros declined, but his gesture meant a lot to her. It was the beginning of their friendship. And now their roles are reversed.

Her thoughts turn to the morning at the café when he related his dream. Ros as his judge, complete with creased forehead and bushy eyebrows. At first the image amused her, but then she became intensely uncomfortable—until Grayson said he'd rather have her than anyone else.

"Not as your judge, I hope," she objected.

"Arbiter may be a better word," he responded. "Someone who listens and gives me honest feedback when I ask for it."

"That's not an arbiter, Grayson. That's a friend."

She remembers his reaction: his hand seeking hers and giving it a firm squeeze. He'd never done that before. Ros remembers how emotional she felt. He understands. He's learning what friendship is. And he accepts!

Some days Ros wonders when Grayson will ask about her. They've talked about her photography a bit and he's helped her decide not to accept the Napoleon commission. He's also curious about the lectures she attends. She's told him about the basics of quantum theory, as if she understood half of it. And she's shown him the dragonfly sketchbook; some of her drawings reminded him of Ontario, he said.

But Grayson has never asked about her childhood or why she's come here or whether she's had a man in her life. She's not sure if that bothers her, knowing that talking about it would make her uncomfortable. Maybe the way things are going is fine for now.

More scenes from the past crowd in. This time she sees herself stand in the tiny kitchen. Outside, against the light of dawn, is Ian, raising his sledgehammer high above his head and bringing it down onto a fencepost. She remembers it's before the Wet, as they called the rainy season—it's late October probably.

The steamy restless nights stretch out forever and the days are merciless in their dull luminosity. Occasionally the cloudless haze is interrupted by the promise of rain: impossibly long grumbles of thunder echo somewhere in the distant skies. But the promise will be withdrawn, again and again, rattling tempers and making people unpredictable. Kids are crashing stolen cars into palm trees, wives walk out on husbands who haven't been home for days. At in the normally mind-numbing, lifeless pub the men drink more and get into fights. Yet here outside the window is Ian, oblivious to all the tension or making the best of it, working away at the fences.

"Take out a cup to him," her mother is saying to her, nodding at the worker outside, pouring tea. And her father chimes in, "A hot cup o' will help 'im stay cool." Ros hides her eagerness to go outside but when she walks up to Ian she feels awkward. He puts down his sledge, wipes his sweaty palms against the denim of his pants and accepts the mug, all along looking into her eyes.

Nearly another month goes by before the rains are near and now bringing tea to Ian has become an early morning ritual. Each time Ros hands him his cup there's that stare again, unflinching, severe and uncomfortably long, but now Ros recognizes Ian's want and allows her eyes to respond.

One day lighting stretches from the horizon to the roof of the purplish black sky and the thunder no longer rolls but comes in vehement claps that make her heart stand still. Ros remembers: you can smell the Wet but it's still not here. It takes its time rolling in across the savanna and now the wait irks even more.

The deluge to come will change everything. Oceans will be hurled at the parched, craggy soil and cause floods that won't recede for weeks, leaving back roads littered with abandoned cars and fields blemished by drowned half-rotted cattle. Peoples' mood will change amidst such carnage. The cursed heat will have passed, but now they'll be trapped in their houses, scratching mildew off radios, tabletops and even cutlery.

Ian comes around to talk. He tells her dad he's quitting and later, behind the house, he tells Ros he's returning to Melbourne. He says she'd like it there.

Ros has little recollection of the endless train ride to the other end of Australia other than that she slept away most of it. But arriving in Melbourne, that she remembers well. The enormous railway station filled with more people than she'd seen or met in her eighteen years put together, and Ros carrying her small suitcase in one hand and holding the worn sheet of paper with Ian's address in the other.

Then the roar of surf surrounds her and she sees Ian on his board, his dark skin glistening and the white of the breaking wave looking flat by contrast. For a moment she lets herself be lost in the intensity of the craving she felt, and then she decides to cut it off.

She picks up the Hasselblad sitting on top of her dresser and points it to her deck and the mountain behind it. She's here now and Australia is the past. Ros focuses the lens and releases the shutter. And then she says aloud, "Here. In Aspen."

But once the mind is engaged it has a life of its own and soon her thoughts return to the past. She catches herself saying, Grayson wouldn't betray me like that, but then abruptly dismisses the thought. Grayson is married and Grayson is a friend. Besides, she can tell that Grayson isn't interested in her that way. What was she thinking?

Yet there is something undeniably forceful that's pulling them together. That she's told him about her woes is meaningless. The morning she broke her tooth and lost her apartment she was so agitated she would have complained to anyone. But Grayson trusting her with his story, that's different.

Lately he's been talking about the time after his accident. His inability to adjust and the therapist who managed to calm him. About coming to terms with what happened and about healing and starting over.

3

GRAYSON HATES IT. HE HAS trouble accepting most things these days, but his loathing for the hospital has reached an intensity he didn't think he was capable of. Not only because he may be stuck in it, but even more so because of the terrifying and predictable mediocrity of all hospitals—the personnel a deplorable collection of automatons, the patients contemptible in their spiritless submission, the edifice a warren of impersonal corridors and recesses painted in badly mixed pastels.

He can tolerate the therapeutic staff and some days he even thinks he likes them. There's Dmitri, the fellow who tries to exercise Grayson's unwilling limbs each morning and afternoon. Grayson can understand the young Russian's purpose and appreciates his effort. He can deal with Sharon Bailey too, although he has a hard time keeping his temper when she pushes him.

Grayson is observing Sharon now. She's sitting across from him reviewing notes inside an oddly slim file bearing his name. Above the tag pinned to her hospital suit saying S. BAYLEY - THERAPY is a slender neck, a well-proportioned face and a mass of raven hair tied up in a bun with no more than an elastic. It would be easy to underestimate her.

Grayson wonders why she doesn't seem interested in making

herself look good. Perhaps she's never learned the skill and perhaps she doesn't care. He thinks of a third possibility: that her appearance at work is deliberately understated. His mind runs free with images of a different Sharon, picturing the fullness of her hair, how she'd be dressed if she worked at an office and what she would wear on a date and when going to bed.

Sharon looks up and her expression says, I bet you're up to no good, and Grayson lowers his gaze to the floor where he sees her white shoes with the conspicuous beige rubber soles.

"What's on your mind, Jack?" Sharon now asks.

"You don't want to know."

"It's my job to know," she says with good humor. "And besides, I'm curious."

For an instant Grayson is holding back, embarrassed, but a sense of irritation overcomes him. "Since you insist," he starts, and Sharon can already gauge from his voice what his state of mind is. It's the Grayson she knows as prickly, as opposed to the one who's angry and speaks from a place way back in his throat. "I was wondering why someone with a great body would wear an outfit that makes them look tubby and overweight."

Sharon looks at him pensively, then says, "You mean it makes *me* look overweight. Tubby, as you call it."

"Yes, you. And those shoes."

Sharon considers again, then laughs. "I suppose you've just paid me a compliment. You did say great body, didn't you?"

"You're very attractive. That suit doesn't do justice to you." The edge has gone from Grayson's voice. He feels awkward now.

Sharon changes the conversation. "Thank you, Jack, that's nice of you." She raises her head, looks at the bit of sky that's visible through the window behind Grayson's head and adds, as if dwelling on a distant memory of early mornings spent in front of a mirror and days complicated by the need to maintain an appearance, "About the baggy green jumpsuit and the seniors' shoes. They're actually very comfortable." Then she gets up from her chair and steps back a couple of feet. "Let's get going with our therapy now, Jack. I'd like you to try something new."

Grayson feels let down. Even if he hasn't enjoyed it, he's been able to direct the conversation for a few moments. Now he's being asked to follow someone else's script again, to surrender the one thing he still has, his mind. "Like what?" he snaps resentfully.

"Something that'll help you find yourself."

"I know who I am, Sharon."

"Oh? Tell me then."

"My name is anger."

"No, Jack. The anger is not you. It's what consumes you." She says this like a kindly schoolteacher who's unhurriedly explaining a historical fact.

Grayson gets irritated. "Trust me, that's all there is."

"And what happens when you get angry? Think of yourself in that state. Evoke the anger feeling and be with it for a moment. Then tell me what happens."

Grayson struggles.

"Come on, I think you know the answer," Sharon prods.

"Never mind."

"All right, let me guess. At best, you feel a temporary surge of energy, or control—followed by what?"

"I don't know." Grayson annoyance is growing, but he's curious where's she's taking this.

"Yes, you do. What follows an explosion of anger isn't what was there before, is it? What follows, Jack? Is it satisfaction?"

"Maybe for a second."

"And then?"

"Feeling heavy, I guess."

"Yes. Alienation with who you are. Perhaps regret that you've diminished someone. Is that right?"

"That does happen, yes."

"And that's the best outcome. Sometimes, what follows anger is much worse."

"What do you mean?"

"What happened two days ago, Jack?"

"The seizure."

"Yes, you get seizures. Episodes, as they call them here."

"The doctors don't link that to anger. They say it's my cerebral cortex."

"The temporal lobe of your cortex is where your form of epilepsy starts. But that's a scientific explanation, which is why doctors love it."

"And what's yours?"

"My view is that the trauma you experienced caused something in your temporal lobe to change. And that you now have to learn to understand how your temporal lobe works."

"What are you getting at?"

"What I'm getting at is the trigger. Something sets off your episodes. Something makes that gasoline smell come on, makes your brain lose control of your hands. What could that something be, Jack?"

"You've already told me. You think it's my anger."

Sharon considers. "It's one likely candidate. There may be others. Look, your seizures must be worse than anything. You're working each day at regaining control of your body, and each time these things overcome you you're thrown back to complete helplessness. It's physically and mentally devastating."

"It's what I may have to live with—that's what Henderson said."

"Doctor Henderson is one of the best surgeons in the country, but as I said, his perspective is purely scientific."

"And what's yours?"

"My goal is to help you heal. With the emphasis on *help*. Most of the healing you have to do yourself."

She notices the frown on Grayson's face but decides to continue. "For starters, try to observe the emotional state you're in. Keep track of your mood swings. Perhaps there is that one thing that triggers your seizures."

All Grayson says is, "Christ."

"Today I'd like to explore only one question, Jack. What do you think causes your anger?"

Sharon watches Grayson's face. He appears to ponder her question, then gives up. In an instant, his expression hardens and his eyes flash hostility.

"Something is bothering you, Jack."

"You're damned right something is bothering me. And I bet you know exactly what it is." Grayson's words sound gruff now, as if it pained him to get them out. "The central question is this, Sharon Bailey. Why me? Why the fuck me?"

"You mean why is it you this happened to?"

"Yes, why me? Here I was, a good husband and father. Never cheated on my wife. Worked hard to keep the family comfortable. Put in extra hours. Oh, there were other guys who fucked around, took sick days and played golf. But not me. I worked, for Christ's sake, and on my way home from work I got shot and ended up a fucking cripple. Why me and not one of those other jerks. Explain that to me!"

Sharon lets seconds tick by before she quietly responds. "I can't explain that, Jack."

"Then at least you've got a reason."

"A reason for what?"

"A reason why I'm burning up inside and why I get my damned seizures!"

Again, Sharon Bailey lets time come between Grayson's words and her response. "Jack, what if we could find a way to keep the seizures away. Wouldn't that be worth trying for?"

Grayson looks at her defiantly.

She moves closer to him, crouches down in front of his wheelchair and reaches up to him. She takes his hands and feels their tension and Grayson's struggle over whether he should allow her. "Look, you're cynical. And angry." Her voice is soft, a whisper as seductive as it is unwavering. "Jack, inside that armor there's a real you. There's kindness and love in there, I know it. And if you want, I'll help you find it."

Grayson stares at her eyes, which are like liquid mirrors reflecting the promise of life itself. He can't hold her gaze.

Tears start trickling down his cheeks. He can tell that Sharon believes in him, like the child nurse Celia did. But while Celia was the embodiment of softness and innocence, his therapist is driven by experience and steely determination.

Over and over, she pushed Grayson to the edge and then withdrew just before he exploded into anger. At first it unsettled him, then he started studying her technique, trying to predict its rhythm. Now he admires her, knowing how good she is at it, understanding how long she must have worked with unhinged and volatile people like him. And what amazes Grayson most is that he's starting to pay attention to Sharon's message. Something in him wants to know whether there is more than anger.

His first mediation class leaves him disoriented. He expects some elusive mixture of mysticism and gymnastics and wonders how he'll be able to participate. Others in his small group have similar misgivings. They've come because their daily routine of therapy and being confined to a wheelchair has left them stone bored, or because like Grayson they've started to wonder about themselves.

The elderly teacher comes right to the point. "What is meditation?" he says, as he closes the door behind him and strides forward toward the six people who make up his class. He's short but holds his body upright like a soldier. His voice is soft. "It's not a religion, it's not a cult and it's not a physical exercise—unless you decide to make it one of these things." He looks at his students one by one and waits.

"An experiment with the mind…is that it?" an overweight young woman asks irritably.

"Well, we could take hallucinogenic mushrooms or LSD but that wouldn't be meditation. We'll get there without resorting to any outside help or stimulation." He grabs one of the folding chairs stacked against the wall, opens it up and sits down. Then he looks at the woman who's challenged him.

"I still don't understand," she says.

He pulls his chair forward so that he sits right in front of her. "Okay, let's try something. I'd like you to close your eyes now and breathe. Take in a healthy deep breath through your nose. Then let it go out again, exhaling through your mouth. Do it five, six times over."

The woman does as she's told. Her breathing is unexpectedly loud. When she opens her eyes again the teacher asks everyone in the group to do the same thing. "Do what you always do," he says quietly. "Breathe in and out, but do it more consciously."

He watches them close their eyes, breathe a few times, then open their eyes again. Then he looks at the circle of wheelchairs around him and turns to Grayson. "Tell me, do you remember what you thought about while breathing?"

"What—when I had my eyes closed?"

"Yes, what were your thoughts?"

"Christ. There was a whole bunch of stuff."

"A whole bunch of stuff. Was there anything you won't mind sharing?"

Grayson reflects. "No, it's okay, I don't mind. Just irrelevant things. Like the faces of the group and you sitting on that chair. And whether I was breathing right. And why I was here, too."

"You thought all that—what, in six or so breaths?"

"Yeah." Grayson grins embarrassedly.

"Thank you." The teacher turns back to the group. "You see, that's the problem we all have. Our brain generates so many impulses that we find it difficult to stick with any one thought. And keeping our mind completely still, without any thought intruding, seems impossible. But that's exactly what we're going to attempt. We'll breathe and let our mind do nothing except follow each breath along its way. In…all the way in. And then out again, slowly. In and out. Breathing will be our technique to help calm the mind. And eventually to empty it."

Grayson reflects on how perplexed he was the first few times he tried. More thoughts than he believed he was capable of crowded in during the space of only a few breaths. What seemed a ridiculously simple task turned out to be one of the most difficult things he'd ever tried.

Yet, while most dropped out of the group, Grayson prevailed. In time he got better. After three weeks he managed to keep out any thoughts for the space of ten, perhaps fifteen breaths. And a few months later he realized he could retreat into a meditative state at will.

In time, his seizures occurred less often, making him believe that anger was a trigger. But there was something else at work too, something he could never understand. Something that severed him from reality once or twice a year, no matter what his emotional state, or how often he meditated, or what medication he was on.

And now, with two recent episodes in a matter of days, the question of what that something is has taken on new urgency.

"AH, BACK TO YOUR NORMAL routine, Grayson," Ros says, as she puts down his cappuccino. "Samantha at the spa again?"

"What are you getting at?"

"You've only been here in the afternoons since your wife got back. Now you're on schedule again." Ros walks over to the counter and says something to Anna, her assistant, then comes back. "Got time for a chat?"

Grayson nods.

"Look," she says, opening her mouth and pointing. "A brand-new tooth. In addition to my stable new accommodation."

"Life is good, I see."

"Yes, Grayson. But I've missed our mornings."

"Me too. I'll be back on schedule for a while." Grayson takes his spoon and scoops off the part of the foam he likes best, the bit in the middle with the cinnamon and muscovado sugar on it.

"A while?"

"About ten days. And then it's off to Denver for a long weekend."

"What's in Denver?"

"A good hotel, but the real destination is Boulder. Don't even ask."

"Okay I won't." But she keeps looking at him.

Grayson holds her gaze for a while, before breaking into a grin. "All right, ask."

"What?"

"Ask me what I'm going to do in Boulder."

But Ros gets up, saying she has to leave him for a moment. Grayson turns and sees one of the town clerks placing his order. He's getting coffee and snacks for several of his colleagues. Behind him, three middle-aged men in matching sheepskin coats and Stetsons are studying the selections on the blackboard and muttering to each other.

He watches Ros take charge, telling Anna to look after the food, while she'll handle the beverages. Grayson notices the newspaper someone has left on the empty chair next to his—the Denver Post this time. He starts reading about Libya and its rivalling factions, then turns away, disgusted. We've done it again, he reflects—invaded in the name of democracy and created something far worse than what was in place before. America and its brainless vassals, keeping yet another nation off balance.

He feels a surge of irritation, but a series of bangs, clangs and piercing hisses from behind the counter intervene. He can only see Ros' head and shoulders, but the sounds guide him through her motions. For a few moments, everything and everyone in the café stops existing. There's only Ros' presence, and as he realizes that a swell of contentment surges through him. They might have been a long-married couple, Grayson sitting at the kitchen table, lamb's wool slippers on his feet, watching Ros through a half-open door sorting through a clothes drawer or folding laundry.

And then she's sitting next to him again, asking him what's in Boulder.

"A seer," he says.

"Come on, Grayson. You mean a psychic?"

"That's not what they're called anymore, Ros. Soothsayer, clairvoyant, fortune-teller, psychic, mystic and medium—all that stuff's out. Samantha assures me that 'seer' is the only acceptable term these days."

"Your Samantha. She's up to mischief again."

"She thinks it'll help me spiritually."

Ros can tell that he wants to say more but has decided against it. For a while they watch the snowflakes dance by the window and then Grayson abruptly gets up, saying he has to leave.

Outside he walks for half a block, then, on the other side of Main Street, breaks into a light jog. Through the fog that hangs behind the snowflakes he can see a dull winter sun. He feels badly about getting up and walking out on Ros, but he was on the verge of talking about Samantha and that's something he's vowed not to do.

In his other life he would have thought of it as merely unprofessional or indiscreet but now there's a lot more to it. Talking to Ros about his marriage would be a betrayal. It would open the trapdoor on which he and Samantha have been standing for the past few years.

Grayson realizes he's hitting a wall with Ros, and no sooner has he completed that thought he knows that he's hitting a wall with Samantha as well. "I'm walled in," he hears himself say aloud, surprised at the matter-of-fact sound of his voice and the lack frustration in it.

The sun breaks through the fog, harsh as halogen against the wall of dark clouds that stands in front of the horizon. Bits of iridescent snow swirl from the rooftops.

As he jogs toward his house Grayson allows the competing voices of his mind to engage, considering each fragment and hoping that it will add something to an irresistibly logical whole. He hears many voices, each presenting its arguments in different ways, using compelling similes and drawing on texture he can easily relate to. But in the end there are only two and Grayson is back where he started. One voice says, if I go further with Ros I'll subvert my marriage. The other, harsh and authoritative in its simplicity, asks back, what marriage?

Grayson settles down for his meditation, rolling out the small rug he keeps in his office. Hendrick Hegedus is on his mind. Now I could use your counsel, Grayson thinks, knowing that the old man's advice would have been cryptic at best. Still, what would Hendrick say?

Grayson leans forward until his head touches the rug. As he breathes in his nose registers the dryness of the wool. He contemplates Hendrick Hegedus and as always, the image of him lying on his deathbed comes first. Grayson tells him how much he's missing him and Hendrick dismissively gestures at his spent body and replies "You don't need this. You carry me inside you." Grayson holds the image until complete calm infuses him.

Later he becomes conscious of thoughts chasing through his mind—thoughts accompanied by images of a younger Samantha. She calls herself Sam here at Hendrick's retreat, before falling in love with how Grayson says her name. Samantha. Unrushed but deliberate: Saaah-maaan-thuuu. He hears her tell him, "My dad used to say it just like you," as they make love the first time. And then she wants him to say it over and over.

Grayson moves back on his knees and straightens himself. He concentrates on emptying his mind. His abdomen expands and contracts as he gradually extends the length of each breath. Years ago he found that his natural rhythm was seven counts in and seven counts out, and that's the rhythm he starts to follow now without being conscious of it. But while his breathing follows the script his mind starts to wander again. New images of Samantha dance through his skull. He keeps dismissing them but they cunningly sneak back seconds later.

Grayson resorts to a trick that's worked before: he decides to chant. He closes his eyes and fills his belly with air until it's round in the way some statues show the Buddha. Then he starts to exhale and give his breath sound. He follows the same routine dozens of times, its effortless and perfect pattern giving him refuge from thought.

In time Samantha returns to his mind, but this time not as an unordered onslaught of thought bits but in her condensed, most pure essence. And he suddenly understands what Hendrick's advice would have been.

"There is no right way or wrong way," he would have said. "There are only circumstance and your intention."

"And what should my intention be?" he'd have asked.

"It should be based on what is considerate to all."

If Hendrick taught him one thing, it was that he had to take responsibility. Sharon Bailey and the meditation teacher at the hospital helped him get up. Hendrick taught him that only he could do the walking.

OUTSIDE THE HUGE WINDOW ARE the Caledon Hills near Toronto. Densely wooded ridges hide behind each other like waves would on a well-behaved ocean. Not long ago the unpretentious evergreens at the top were outdone by brash oaks and maples in their autumn best. Closer to the valley troughs you had to fight your way through dense sumac trees which glowed dark red. Now their twisted branches look lonesome and barren. If you continue down still further you'll end up wading through leaves two feet deep but still too shallow to hide the tips of a million rigid stalks. These belong to ferns whose emerald lushness is now memory.

Inside, where Hendrick and Grayson sit opposite each other, the morning sun looks harsh, but its first rays feel remarkably warm. The meditation hall is austere in a way that inspires wonder, much like the blue tinted snow on the other side of its arched windows or the splendid ridges in the distance.

"My problem is anger," Grayson says softly. "And I think I know what causes it."

"Ah." Hendrick's eyes are like pools of truth, luminescent and knowing.

"The anger happens when I feel sorry for myself. But what I need to find out is what's at the root of feeling sorry for myself," Grayson continues.

"How do you think you can find peace, Jack?"

"Probably by meditating."

"Meditation can be a useful tool. Has it worked for you?"

"It's the one thing that allows me to think I can control my mind. And it calms me."

"And that calm? How long does it last?"

Grayson contemplates the question. "Sometimes a minute, sometimes longer. Until the mind starts again. The thoughts want back in." Then he adds awkwardly, "I guess that means I can't control my mind."

"It's good you can see that, Jack." Hendrick closes his eyes. Half a minute goes by before he opens them again and asks, "But tell me more about those thoughts."

This time Grayson takes his time, opening himself to the truth. "Trivial stuff mostly. But somehow fear comes back in. And self-pity. And then I get angry again."

"Fear and self-pity. And anger. They always come back in, don't they?" Hendrick says quietly, and then he waits as Grayson, bombarded by fragments of his past, cries. How proud he was of Marlene, how satisfied with the boys and his position and the house in Rosedale. And he was healthy, never even thought of health as something that wouldn't always be there. And wasn't that true of everything he had? Wasn't that the way he thought of it all? His for always—his because he'd worked for it and was therefore entitled to it.

And now the fragments lie in pieces, shards of a once price-less urn swept into a ditch and on the verge of being erased from memory. His family gone, his influence and position obliterated, and his body shattered. He's nothing now and he has to learn not to be angry about it.

Anger is his ego, he knows that. The part of him that's upset about losing a life he thought of as perfect. Life in the sweet spot!

But anger is also what he's tried to conquer for too long. He's tired of it and he knows it doesn't work. He needs to surrender and wants to surrender, wants to become clay in the hands of his teacher. And thank heaven for Hendrick, who he can see is pure love and who takes an interest in him and can help.

Grayson cries for the injustices he's done to Marlene and Oliver and Martin and weeps for the kindness of those who helped him at the hospital. And as he cries, he realizes that he's still capable of harboring good feelings, feelings of gratitude and humility and kindness, and that makes him cry even more.

When he's done his kerchief is wet from the tears he's shed. Hendrick sits opposite him, where he was before, serene and immobile and exuding a stillness that seamlessly merges with the wintry calm outside. Grayson wishes he could stay in this moment, wrap himself in its precious tenderness like a moth in its silken cocoon.

Soundless seconds pass by. For quite a while, Hendrick Hegedus' eyes keep resting on the wooden floor in front of him. But when he looks up again, they express something that Grayson has never encountered: acceptance and understanding of such magnitude that it transforms into the most condensed form of kindness. Hendrick hasn't said a word, yet Grayson is overwhelmed by love. His eyes fill with tears and for a few seconds he struggles against letting go, but then he opens himself to the little man sitting across from him completely. When he recovers his balance, he looks up at his teacher, whose eyes are trained on the floor again.

"Thank you," Grayson says between sobs. "Thank you."

This time there is no view onto the ridges. The nearby bushes look like stage-sets behind the snow clouds that race past, pressed on by a wind whose chant Hendrick and Grayson can hear as if it were sung inside the hall.

Jack asks, "What can I do to stop it?"

Hendrick lets the question be.

"To keep the thoughts out. What can I do?" Grayson tries again.

"What happens when the thoughts come?" Hendrick gives Grayson space to visualize them, feel them being there. "What do you feel when that happens?"

Grayson considers. "I hate them, I guess. They're awful."

"You hate them." Another long pause follows. "And in your body, what do you feel when the thoughts are there?"

Grayson considers. "Tightness. I feel tightness."

"Can you feel the tightness now?"

Grayson closes his eyes, allows himself to become aware. "Yes," he says softly. "It's there now."

"And what does it feel like, Jack. Can you describe it?"

"My stomach. There are knots to the sides of my navel. And my throat is tight." Grayson's breathing is raspy now, his voice tight. "I want them to go away."

Hendrick lets Grayson be for a while, then asks, "And you've told me how you've tried to make that happen."

"Yes, I can control it. Make them disappear for a few moments. But they come back."

"What if you allowed them to stay, Jack, the thoughts and the emotions they evoke?" The master pauses, as if in his realm only emptiness mattered. "Could you allow them to be without commenting, judging or resisting?"

"You mean right now?"

"Yes, even welcome them in. Would that be okay?"

Grayson weighs the idea. "I suppose I could try it."

"When you think of trying it, what do you feel?"

Grayson says, "Suspicion. Fear that it won't work, I suppose." His face asks for forgiveness, says he's embarrassed by his words, but it's how he feels.

Hendrick's expression remains unchanged, his eyes like two windows reflecting what's outside. Grayson holds them for a second or two, finds the lack of reaction immensely soothing, and locks the image in his heart. Then he lowers his lids and considers what Hendrick has asked him, allowing the idea to spread out. And soon his breathing slows and he thinks his stomach feels a bit less raw. "It's okay, Hendrick" he hears himself say. "It feels a bit better."

"It feels better," Hendrick repeats, his words seemingly taking forever to be said.

Grayson decides to try again. He feels vulnerable, aware of the comforting stillness around him but uneasy about the chaos that may take hold of his mind. He closes his eyes.

Fear makes its entry. Grayson doesn't recognize it at first because it has no voice. It's his mind he hears instead, a reasonable, soft-spoken presence this time, an old friend asking him why he'd ever allow his negative feelings in. Didn't that lead to his seizures? But now, as he hears this, he can feel fear lurking nearby: a cold, menacing presence that's growing even as he contemplates acknowledging it. He reasons with his mind for a while, saying that he must try, because Hendrick is love and Hendrick knows whereas he is utterly confused. And while arguing this way he realizes what's going on and disengages himself from the noisy dialogue.

There is no moment when Grayson speaks words or thoughts specifically inviting fear; it knows all by itself that it can enter and stay. They spend four or five minutes together, Grayson gently assuring it that it's welcome and that it's entitled to its own views, and fear shrinking in size and no longer threatening. To Grayson's surprise, self-pity and anger don't even make an appearance and now he knows: if he doesn't try to control his negative thoughts, they stop fighting for control of him. They turn compliant, seemingly content to just exist.

When eventually he opens his eyes again, Hegedus still sits there, silent and small in stature, but with a presence that would attract millions if they only knew it existed.

Grayson's meditations become longer and he's asked to be assigned some chores. Among other things he's in charge of keeping the courtyard clean. Now in winter, that means shoveling snow, which is a punishing task for him. He can walk only slowly, and lifting the shovel, even with only a small amount of snow on it, strains the part of his back that is giving him all the trouble. In the afternoon he's on kitchen duty, helping the cooks chop vegetables for dinner.

Saturday is most important: that's when Grayson has his weekly meeting with Hendrick.

"I saw you shovelling snow after the storm," Hendrick says

during one of these get-togethers. "You were doing well."

"I think my back is getting better."

"I am glad to hear it, Jack. You look healthy."

"Hendrick, there is something I'd like to ask you about. I know there is a time limit to staying here at the retreat."

Hendrick listens.

"I'm at peace here and I'm making good progress. But I feel it's too soon to be leaving."

"How long have you been here now?"

"Just over eight weeks."

"You have another month."

"I wonder if you could make an exception. You've taught me so much. Made me see things differently. I'm scared of leaving here."

Hendrick's eyes rest on Grayson's. Long moments pass. "Everyone is afraid of going back. But you'll be well prepared. Think of what you've learned while staying here."

"Thanks to you, yes."

"No Jack. You must remember that it's you who's progressed along this path. Step by step. All I did was help you see the signposts."

Grayson thinks about Hendrick's words. "I know what you say is true, but still."

"But still?"

"I'm afraid, Hendrick."

"Fear is our constant companion in life. As you already know, trying to conquer it doesn't work, no matter how hard we try. We have to work on accepting it." Hendrick's words roam the expanse of the meditation hall, gliding along the worn floorboards and searching out corners, and Grayson recognizes their wisdom and understands their finality. For a long while, the two men sit silently, looking at each other.

And then there is a flicker in Hendrick's eyes and he starts to giggle. "Besides, Jack, you'll always be able to come and visit. Maybe we'll even need help with the snow."

AS THEY LEAVE THE CAFÉ they feel the pinch of the cold. They walk fast, hurrying around the corner and down the alley toward the car, when Ros tugs at Grayson's arm and stops.

"Look up," she says, her eyes on the darkening sky. Only the brightest stars are yet visible, still milky in appearance and their edges undefined. "It'll be a new moon tonight. And not a cloud up there."

Then they get into the Highlander, which slips on the ice a few times as they drive downhill toward the river. They leave the car in the lot across from the post office, cross the sturdy bridge and start following the river toward the west end of town.

Grayson breaks the silence. "I'm sorry about this morning, Ros. Running out on you like that." He puts his arm around her shoulder and gives her a squeeze.

"It helped that you phoned."

"Still."

"You should have seen yourself when you got up. Stunned. As if you'd walked into a wall."

"Funny you should use that image. I left the café and literally thought I'm walled in. Those exact words."

Ros considers for a moment before asking, "What's the wall, Grayson?"

"There are two. You are one, Samantha the other."

"I had an inkling it had to do with your wife, but me? How am I a wall, exactly?"

Grayson stops and turns to her. "Maybe I said that badly. What I mean is that I've hit some internal walls. Walls I built. It's not something that you or Samantha have done."

"I see."

"You've been helping me a lot, just listening."

"But there's more, isn't there?"

"What do you mean?"

"More you want me to listen to, no?"

Grayson points to a bench and suggests they sit down, but Ros says she wants to keep moving. For a while they walk on, saying nothing. Even though they are still close to town it's so quiet they can hear the murmur of the river.

When they come to the first of the little walking bridges that span the river, Grayson stops again. "You're right, Ros. There is a lot more I want to talk about. I thought about it all day and this is how it is. On the one hand there is you. You've been wonderfully patient with me and opened my eyes to what friendship can be. Remember how we defined what a friend was?"

"Someone who holds a mirror to your face?"

"Better. Someone who listens and gives honest feedback when asked for it. I've had feedback all my life, but usually of the unsolicited kind or from people who never listened. Or they had an agenda. What you're giving me is much more."

"I'm glad to help, Grayson. Actually, being straight with people has never been a problem for me. Most think me too direct."

"I don't. You've been a model of restraint. Each time I bring up Samantha in our talks, I pull back. And you let me."

"There have been times when you got me curious. Even frustrated."

Grayson guides Ros to the middle of the sloped bridge and they stop to look down. He pushes bits of frozen snow off the railing and watches them disappear. A group of ducks comes swimming toward them, hardly visible against the black water.

"You know how far you can go without pushing me into discomfort, Ros."

"Is that what a good friend does?"

"For a while."

"And then?"

"I guess it's up to me to move on. I've been pissing around long enough, don't you think?"

Ros doesn't reply.

"Come on, Ros. I bet I know what you're thinking right now."

"What?"

"You're thinking, here he goes again with the Samantha topic—let's see how long it'll take him to lose his nerve this time. Am I right?"

"You want to know?"

Grayson considers. "I want you to understand that it's not a problem of nerves."

"Then what is it, Grayson?"

"A rule I made for myself. That I wouldn't start discussing Samantha."

Ros links her arm into his and looks up at him. "But you do want to talk about her, don't you?"

Grayson sees her sincerity and loves her for it. And as her eyes move back to the water, he sees something else: her beauty. Her face is flushed from the cold and bits of breath come from her lips and evaporate into the winter evening and he knows how satisfying it would be to kiss her. He's never allowed himself to think of her this way before and he starts to wonder what it means. And as he does so her eyes meet his again and he sees the flicker of embarrassment as she turns her head. She's read his thoughts.

"I've wanted to talk about lots of things, since we started this. It's like a floodgate that's opened," he tries.

"But?"

"But Samantha. She's a good person."

"Ah, loyalty."

"Mixed with guilt, maybe. I'm not sure, Ros. I've always been faithful to her."

"I suspected. You've never said anything negative about her. Apart from mild complaints about her spa trips."

"And her wanting me to be more spiritual, as she calls it." He turns away from the bridge, feeling better.

"I wasn't sure whether that was a joke."

"Not to her. She thinks that the seer will put me more closely in touch with my inner self."

"I guess that's possible."

"For Samantha, the possibilities are endless."

They start walking again, brisker this time. Grayson looks at his watch but it's too dark to see what time it is.

"Look, Samantha is out with the girls tonight. Their mid-week ritual. Do you want to have dinner with me?"

"Can we go to the Mexican place?"

"If I can find a way to keep you away from the Margaritas."

For a few minutes they stand waiting, glad to be inside the warm restaurant and soaking up its bubbly atmosphere. Waitresses carrying steaming dishes and frosted beer mugs squeeze by and a mariachi tune blasts from the overhead speakers. When they're shown to a table Grayson has to dodge the strings of flashing lights hanging from the ceiling.

They order drinks—a Margarita for Ros and a Diet Coke for Grayson.

"Let's get back to our conversation," Ros leads. "I want to know about the other wall."

"The one I built between us?"

"Yeah, that one."

"I'm not sure. I guess there's a beam somewhere linking the two walls."

"Now you sound like an engineer, Grayson. I'm not sure I can follow that."

Grayson can't hear; a vocal tune booms from the low ceilings, the voice aggravatingly shrill. Ros repeats, shouting, "I said you sound like an engineer."

Grayson throws up his hands and waits for the voices to subside. He leans forward. "My overwhelming desire is to talk to you, Ros. About everything: Samantha, my father, the lot. I guess I want to open up to you completely. But I feel I should first make some decisions about my marriage. And there's something else. I'm not sure why you."

"What do you mean—why me?"

"Why it's you I want to open up to."

"Maybe it's because I'm a good listener. A friend."

"Maybe. And maybe there's more."

"Like what?"

"I don't know. I've been feeling very comfortable with you. There are times when I think I can let my guard down completely, make myself vulnerable. And when I actually do, it feels good."

Grayson sees the girl with the drinks come their way and stops. She puts the Margarita in front of him and hands the pop across the table to Ros. Then she asks what she can bring them to eat. Grayson says they need more time.

Miraculously, the music stops in mid-tune.

"Here's to a moment of quiet," Ros says. "And to making ourselves vulnerable." She toasts him with his Coke, while Grayson holds up her Margarita. They clink and then switch glasses.

"You think that's a good thing?" Grayson asks.

"Vulnerability?" Ros considers. "There are times I get frustrated with you—sometimes it pisses me off when you go three quarters of the way, then clam up. But then I reflect on what's happened and find myself wishing I could open up the way you do."

Grayson considers Ros' words, then laughs. "Open up the way I do? I think that needs some context."

"What do you mean?"

"Well, just consider that I know about four people in all of Aspen after several years here. And it was the same during my career years in Toronto. I had to interact professionally, of course, but Marlene and I had no social life to speak of. That's partly because revealing myself is not something I'm comfortable with." Grayson throws up his hands, then adds, "And yet, somehow it feels right with you. Now I have to figure out why."

"Grayson, let's make a deal, okay?"

"Tell me."

"Why don't you pretend you're talking to me because we're

friends and that's all. I'm not sure what other possibilities you have on your mind but I suspect I'm not ready for them. Walls of my own, you know."

"So I talk and you listen?"

"Like we've done so far. As friends."

"And what if there's more?"

"We'll deal with that as it comes. But for now you have too much on the go." Ros puts her hand on his. "Think about your marriage, Grayson, and what you want to do with that part of your life. Share your thoughts with me when you feel the time is right. What do you say?"

Grayson isn't satisfied, but when he reflects on Ros' words, he can't dispute her wisdom or the generosity of her offer. After a while he responds, raising his glass. "To friendship," he says.

GRAYSON FINDS IT EASY TO move in the dark. His accident and being in a wheelchair vastly improved his sensory perception. In the hospital he noticed he could overhear his neighbor's whispered phone conversations. And his vision and sense of smell got pushed to the edge of possibilities.

Nothing's changed since. He can hear a tap dripping at the other end of the house and knows when someone thirty feet away breaks a fart. And sometimes his senses offer him experiences that don't exist.

There's the tingling of his teeth. Before being shot he would have dismissed the notion that teeth can do that, but that's what happens to him now when he's agitated.

Tonight, Grayson is unaware of what state he's in. He ably navigates his way through the impenetrable dark and slips into bed. But once he lies back on his pillow his teeth tell him. They tingle, much as an elbow does when its funny bone is hit, except it's not unpleasant. He's smelled Samantha in the hallway, but now her scent descends on him like dew settles on a dawn meadow. It enters him, first through his nostrils and then through every pore; and once inside, the myriad messengers of his nervous system carry it to each of his cells. He takes deep breaths to calm himself but doing so allows the sweet-sour scent to enter at an even faster rate. He tries to define it, deconstruct the blended aroma: citrus, musk, lemongrass, a hint of leather even. Grayson wonders if Ros' skin is fragrant the way Samantha's is. He's surprised he's never noticed.

The darkness of the bedroom is absolute. Even he of the perfect night vision can't see Samantha in this chamber of black liquid, but he pictures her lying near him. He knows she looks stunning, even in her pyjamas and with her make-up removed. She's hardly changed.

Grayson recalls the way everyone looked at Sam when she checked into Hendrick's retreat. He sees her entering the mediation hall wearing jeans and a white sweater, her hair closely cropped. He's wondering if its straw color is natural and at that precise moment she turns to him and looks straight at him as though he were the only person in the room.

Two weeks go by and each time she's there he seeks her eyes again and she his, but still they don't speak to each other. When finally she sits down next to him one day at dinner time he's nervous. Dealing with people is a challenge for him. He's afraid of his anger. The only thing that's given him refuge from his inner chaos is meditation. Hendrick's exercises calm his soul and give him strength. He's been at the retreat for fourteen weeks and wishes he'd never be asked to leave.

The following day Sam sits next to him again and soon it becomes a habit. He's thankful the retreat has rules. There are parts of the day—and mealtime is among these—when they aren't allowed to talk, and so the rituals of a joint supper become the instruments of communication. When he silently offers to fill her soup bowl she holds it out a little longer than necessary.

Grayson anxiously waits for that moment. It gives him time to look into her eyes.

There's another rule at the retreat: they can't talk of the past or the future, except to Hendrick. The idea is to live in the now. And so, when Sam and Grayson start to go for walks together they talk of the beauty that surrounds them here. Or what they're reading. Or Hendrick. And even though they don't comprehend anything about each other's origin they know enough to become friends.

One afternoon, sitting with Sam on a pile of leaves still left from fall and watching mauve evening clouds drift by, Grayson feels an erection. The doctor said that would never happen again. Just then Sam says it's too cold to sit and suggests they walk for a bit. And when he reluctantly gets up, she notices his discomfort and her expression changes to one of wonderment at what may be and she tells him she feels the same way about him.

Lying in the dark next to his sleeping wife Grayson watches the string of images in which the two of them became one—their touches cautious at first and their kisses tenderly probing. Later the intensity of lovemaking and after that, as they lay caressing each other, the awakening of a hope that said they now had each other and surely the energy of their love would eat away at the despair and anxiety that had been with them for so long.

Grayson remembers lying on the bed of wilted leaves for what seemed an eternity before becoming aware of the bite of early winter's cold. Sam is shivering as they start to walk back toward the retreat and he holds her tightly. They're unaware of the roots and rocks over which they stumble in their excitement. Grayson marvels at their frequent stops to touch and kiss more, drunk on their newly found desire, and as he contemplates these images others impatiently crowd in. He feels love infuse him, not just for

Sam but for the world, and he sees them talk about leaving the retreat. Then there's the scene where they sit in front of Hendrick together, and next they return to the world.

Grayson recalls their vow to each other: not to allow themselves to hope for anything. They also understood that visiting the past bore risks; dwelling there could derail their fledgling love.

But things turned out well. Sam's soul was as bruised as his. She often cried about her father, telling Grayson how his death had destroyed her mother. She'd become overbearing and intolerant, then repressive, and one day kicked her twenty-year old daughter out of the house. Sam moved in with friends and turned to drugs.

In time Grayson told Samantha about his hurt and how the meditation classes at the hospital and Sharon Bailey and Hendrick had helped.

Together, soothing and cuddling each other and clinging to a rigid routine of meditation, they coped. They left their apartment only occasionally and hardly ever alone. As individuals they were still dysfunctional.

Grayson reaches for the water bottle on his night table and drinks. He feels calmer now, but his teeth are still acting up. He turns sideways and snuggles up to Samantha's warmth. We've come a long way, you and I, he thinks to himself. But somewhere we've taken a wrong turn. Neither of us can be blamed, but that doesn't make things better.

The dream again. The silently closing stainless steel doors when the elevator leaves his floor and the soft whoosh as it stops again. Grayson sees the red sign above flashing 34. When he lowers his eyes again the Fedex driver has his back to him. Grayson thinks of saying something, both to apologize to the man and to get a look at his face, but he knows his mouth is so dry he won't be able to open it. The elevator takes a long time to get down.

When Grayson approaches the parking lot the attendant is missing. Maybe that's a good thing because Grayson owes him an apology too. Better to come back when he can talk.

He feels better when he sees his car, immaculately polished and parked in the same spot as always. He takes off his jacket, opens the door and slides in, his right hand caressing the doe-skin passenger seat and then joining the left on the rosewood steering wheel.

At the gas pump he chuckles as he keeps pressing the green "on" sign at the pump, knowing it's good for him to do ordinary things. It keeps him in touch with regular life. But when he looks at his hand and sees the white film the evaporating gasoline has left on his palm and down the sides of his fingers, he knows what's next. He starts feeling sick, gasoline fumes overwhelming him.

The men are still inside the booth. Any moment now they'll come out.

When he sees them Grayson gets confused. One of them is Sam as she appeared at the retreat: her hair blond and short-cropped. But when the arm slowly rises and he sees the pistol at the end of the straight line that points right through him, he knows it's not Samantha.

Grayson cries out as he spins forward, his arms holding on to the side of his Lexus. In front of his eyes is a fiery speck of energy and it takes him a moment to understand that this is the evening sun bouncing off his car window. Next, he watches his hands slide lower and obliterate the fragment of light, and then they are gone too.

For a second or two Grayson stares at the now mucky glass and through it to the dashboard with its polished controls and the sumptuous leather seats below. For some reason Marlene and the boys are inside the car too, which adds to his agony. All he yearns for is condensed into one blazing desire—he's outside and he wants back in.

The Grayson of the past reaches down to open the door, losing the trace of balance he still has and he falls, forever it seems, while the Grayson who's dreaming realizes what that means. Even if he's allowed to live all will be impermanent from here on, the constancy he's treasured gone, his plans for the future exposed as a spiteful tease, and all hope blotted out by pain and anger.

Grayson screams and screams, until he hears a voice. Someone's trying to tell him he's okay. The odor of gasoline and the sour stink of his fear are still there but he's aware of a pleasant scent as well. His back is being lifted and a hand is behind his head. The medics probably.

Then he hears Samantha: "You're dreaming, Jack. Everything is fine, darling."

He lies in her arms exhausted, sweat pouring down his face, and wonders how he could ever leave her.

"Come and have breakfast, Jack," Samantha calls.

Grayson walks over to the kitchen to tell her he'll shower first, but changes his mind. "Let me grab a towel, at least." He goes to the cooking island, takes a dish towel from a drawer and wipes his face.

"Jack, not with the linen," Samantha protests, then gives up and laughs. "I can't believe you went jogging. You must be exhausted after last night."

"I always jog, Samantha." He kisses her on the cheek. "Thanks for rescuing me from my dream."

"Bad one, huh?"

"Same as always. The gas station, getting shot, sliding down the side of the car. That's the worst part, that last one where I'm locked out of the life I had."

"Here, have some sheep's milk ricotta. Fresh from Italy. It's fabulous on toast."

Grayson walks over to the toaster and places two slices of bread in it. "I've always dreamed, you know."

"What do you mean?"

"I mean before the accident I had dreams as well. But they were different, then. The one I must have had a hundred times had me flying, invariably in the twilight of dawn or dusk, effortlessly navigating the currents, a deserted pristine earth extending below me. Gently rolling hills, some of them covered by juicy meadows and some by lush forests—that kind of thing. Landing was never part of the movie; not once did I touch down on a tree limb to rest. And never could I figure out what I was."

"A bird, I imagine?"

"Well, I couldn't see myself as I was gliding, wings outstretched and legs retracted. A bird, yes. But was I a raven, an eagle, a hawk? What I remember is the boundless joy I felt as I was gliding, tempered only by the knowledge that I'd have to wake up."

"That's beautiful, Jack."

"Yes. The air that carried me was timeless and inescapable, so why was it that I couldn't keep flying forever?"

Samantha was polishing her knife with a linen napkin. "Can you believe this dishwasher? Top of the line and it still leaves water stains."

"I felt so strong then, Samantha. In complete control. Everything seemed possible." He brings the toast, sits down and helps himself to cheese and a fresh fig. "And look at me now."

"Would you be a darling and hand me the grapes?"

Grayson passes her the hand-painted bowl. "What do you dream about these days, Samantha?"

"I don't dream much, Jack. Isn't this ricotta heavenly?"

"Come on, I'm interested in this. What about when you do have dreams?"

"Oh, I'm on a beach with you and we make love. Or we drive to Boulder together to visit the seer." She giggles.

"When we make love on the beach, how is it?"

"Exquisite. Just the way it was the first time."

"And it's always me. You never make love with strangers?"

"Always you."

Grayson believes her. How easy it would be if she had affairs.

"And you, darling, do you have erotic dreams?"

"No, no love making. My dreams are tedious, excluding the nightmare, that is."

The teapot whistles and Samantha gets up. When she brings their mugs the smell of peppermint hits Grayson's nostrils.

"Here is another. Not as bad as getting shot, but unpleasant nonetheless. When asked to address the board of directors, I suddenly realize my teeth are missing".

"What are you talking about, Jack?" Samantha's eyes are fixed on her iPhone.

"You asked me about my damned dreams, remember?"

"Oh yes, I'm sorry. The dreams."

"Anyway, no teeth. I first tell myself that it's not such a bad thing, provided no one notices."

"How could they not notice?" Samantha asks, while pointing at the basket with toast.

Frustrated, Grayson hands her a slice, wondering when it was that she started getting like this. He's determined to finish his story. "At some point in the dream I realize that talking is actually possible without showing the existence or absence of my teeth. All I have to do is keep my lips close together. The only problem is that I can't smile without exposing myself, and guess what— my fucking smile is the key attribute of my business persona."

Samantha jumps up; her phone has dinged again. "I can hear the frustration in your voice, Jack. Not a nice dream. But I must be going now, my darling, or I'll be late for the gym." She starts walking toward the bedroom, saying how amazing it is that he can function at all.

Grayson watches her disappear and swears to himself. He reflects on the years they've been together, convinced Samantha wasn't always this flighty.

He lets his mind return to the past, to when he first arrived at the retreat, convinced that he'd never again find love of the depth and intensity he'd experienced with Marlene. Theirs was far more than a shared journey—it was a coming together of concern and kindness, respect and integrity. he mumbles to himself. "I had it all," he mumbles to himself. "And then I let my anger fuck it up."

He recalls saying those same words to Hendrick—word he's repeated to himself hundreds of times since. He'd convinced himself that he'd never find love like that again, that the best he could hope for in the future was companionship.

Hendrick had sidestepped the comment, replying that with healing endless possibilities would arise, a perspective Grayson found difficult to accept.

But then Samantha stepped into his life and words became utterly meaningless. Not only was there the prospect that they could comfort each other on their return to a regular life, but there was boundless attraction between them. For a long time, all that mattered was physical closeness, something he'd convinced himself would be unattainable to him. So overwhelming was the surge of excitement of being with Samantha that even the promise of lasting companionship seemed of peripheral importance.

But that surge has been gone for some time, Grayson muses. And then he asks himself if he's giving up on Samantha, before resolutely dismissing the thought.

His hand moves across the linen tablecloth toward a few leftover crumbs. As he pulls them together, he's surprised with what ease the hard-baked dark bits attach themselves to the white doughy morsels. Eventually a perfect orb forms under Grayson's index, but he keeps going, relentlessly rolling the crumb ball as if doing so could turn it back into something useful.

AS THE SUN RISES OVER Glenwood Canyon the riverbank next to the highway comes to life. Trees that have looked dull moments before glisten with life, and the sparse grasses between them turn into a carpet of light. The sunlight changes the water too, turning the grey swirls yellow and the wave caps silver.

Grayson keeps looking at Samantha periodically, checking if she's still asleep. Another half hour and they'll be at their breakfast spot in Silverthorne. He looks forward to his Western Omelette and to talking with Samantha. They can have a conversation. There's nowhere she'll have to run to, here in the middle of Interstate 70, nothing she needs to do. Perhaps this is the way to restore their relationship. Go on trips together. Grayson realizes that Samantha has suggested just that so many times. Maybe she's as conscious of what they've lost as he is. Maybe he is the problem.

Outside the restaurant, he reaches over to Samantha and gently shakes her. She looks up at him drowsily and says, "Be a darling, Jack, and bring me some orange juice when you come back."

"What, you're not coming in?"

"Make sure it's not the stuff from concentrate." Her eyes are closed again.

Back on the highway Grayson thinks they'll have an opportunity to talk when they get to Boulder, but as they arrive at the hotel Samantha informs him that she's booked a beauty treatment.

Only at dinner do they finally have a chance to talk. He asks Samantha whether she's excited about the seer.

"Of course I am, Jack. Louise Bernstein says he's booked for months ahead. Do you know whose spot we got? Fred Merkle's, that's who."

"Who the hell is Fred Merkle?"

"Jack, darling. The painter! Remember the piece we considered buying?"

"Oh yeah, that big red thing. Anyway, how do you know?"

"Louise told me after she booked us. Just imagine."

Grayson stabs at his meal, trying to think of what they can talk about. "Who should go first?" he tries.

"You of course, Jack."

"Why of course?"

"Don't be silly. If I go first, you'll be skeptical."

"Huh?"

"You'll think I've told him things about you."

"Oh, I see. That's a good point."

"I know, darling. You'd never do this on your own. I know it's a favor."

"Samantha, what if we did this kind of thing together more often? Going away places, I mean."

She puts down her cutlery and leans across the table, extending her lips in a pretend kiss. "Jack, I can't believe you said this. I'd love for you to come to the spa with me. Or we could visit that ashram Judy Vidal goes to. I'd love for us to do that together. It would be like at the retreat, Jack!"

"I wasn't thinking of spas and ashrams so much."

"But why not? We must keep searching, Jack."

"I thought it would be nice to talk more. At home we never seem to do that."

"We can talk anywhere."

"It would be difficult to talk with mediation classes, quiet times and spa treatments going on."

"Jack, we used to be into this thing together. Remember Hendrick's retreat? That's where we fell in love; it was the basis from which our relationship evolved. What happened to that?"

Grayson ponders the question. He sees the two of them at a silent meal in the dining hall of the retreat. He thinks of the tiny apartment they first had together.

"I liked that simplicity, Samantha."

"I still like the way you say my name, Jack."

"How can we go back there?"

"You mean to Hendrick's place? He's dead, darling. Things change. We can't go back to what once was."

"Well something else that's simple, then."

"Like what?"

"It doesn't matter, really, as long as there are no prescribed activities. We could go to Sicily or drive through the Pyrenees. Maybe stay at small guest houses."

"Oh, now you make me think about Marbella. You won't believe who's there every summer. I bet you someone we know has a boat there. That's what I really miss here, the water."

"I'd like to be with *you*, Samantha, not with the social set, and definitely not cooped up on a yacht with others."

"But you'd have a good time, I promise. You know most of them."

"Yes I do. But I want to be with you. Alone, in a place where we can communicate."

"Communicate?" There's panic in Samantha's voice now and tears are forming in her eyes. "You know, we didn't talk all that much when we were with Hendrick. It was a silent retreat, for God's sake. And later, before we came here, we meditated together and read. We were happy to have that in common. We didn't have to discuss it." She's dabbing her face with the napkin.

"That's true, I guess."

"Jack, let's be realistic. What's in the Pyrenees that we don't have right here in the Rockies? And what would we do in Sicily?"

"Sit in small restaurants overlooking magnificent seascapes, sipping espresso. Watch fishermen mend their nets. Take in the local teenagers buzzing by on scooters."

"I'm happy where I am, Jack. I have my friends and we have lots of things in common. I'm content to be here, but when I think of going away, what comes to mind first are the spas and ashrams I've always wanted to visit." Samantha's tears flow freely now. "It's not that I haven't asked you join me. But you keep telling me it's not your thing."

"Samantha, I'm trying to tell you something. It's you I want. Not the ashram and not your crowd."

"Jack, we can have good times as things are. We have a good life the way things are. What would we be doing together if it were just the two of us, all the time?"

"We could start by talking."

"Well, isn't that what we're doing? I mean, what more is there to say?"

Grayson is at a loss for words.

The waiting room is sparse. Grayson has imagined an upstairs location with small windows in which colorful lights spelling words like PSYCHIC and TAROT and YOUR FORTUNE READ dangle. Instead, Abelard Pereira's office is next to a legal firm on the 6th floor of one of Boulder's premier buildings.

Samantha announces their arrival in reverential whispers which the receptionist acknowledges with a curt nod. Her glass desktop is empty except for a phone.

Grayson is fascinated by her. She wears an understated black suit that matches her short-cropped black hair. Her skin is like gray-frosted glass and her conspicuous fingernails are white. He imagines what Pereira-Jackman will look like. The image of death in an Ingmar Bergman movie comes to his mind: black-and-white, ascetic. Grayson imagines the exotic sound of his speech, envisions a man in a full-length caftan.

He's wrong. The seer is short, with a fleshy face and a mop of curly hair. He wears a dark blue suit; he could be one of the lawyers down the hall. When he introduces himself as Abel Pereira there isn't the slightest trace of an accent. They shake hands.

Samantha is too excited to think. She says, "Louise Bernstein speaks so highly of you," and holds on to the seer's hand for too long. Pereira seems uncomfortable and asks who wants to join him first.

Samantha giggles. "If you don't mind, my husband. He's a bit skeptical, you know."

The seer's office is as minimalist as the reception: white, black and shades of gray. A series of color prints of zodiac signs makes a bold counterpoint but doesn't take away from the austerity of the room. To the side is Pereira's desk; in the middle stands a small table flanked by two chairs on which the seer and his client now sit.

Grayson waits for something to happen. Since sitting down a few moments ago Pereira has looked at him in the most unusual manner. He's staring, but in an unfocused and benign way, much like a hiker who's climbed to the top of a ridge and now, tired from his effort, lets his eyes gaze over the familiar valley below him.

"I'm sorry if I make you uneasy, Mr. Grayson."

"Is there anything I should do or say?"

"You must wonder what I'm doing," Pereira says. "Your wife makes it sound like you'd rather not be here."

"I *am* here because of her. A favor of sorts."

Pereira simply looks at him, reverting to his imprecise stare.

Grayson starts to feel more relaxed and wonders why. "Actually, I don't mind being here now," he says. "I feel almost comfortable. Don't ask me why."

"What were your reservations when you came here?"

Grayson reflects. "Instinct more than anything. Something telling me it was a waste of time."

"Swindle and chicanery?"

"No, those words are too strong. Less harmful than that. It's the people I imagine coming here that turn me off, not you."

"People who want to be misled, you mean?"

"Yes, I guess that's it."

"Then what does that make me, Mr. Grayson? Someone who misleads?"

Grayson struggles for an answer, then laughs. "I got myself into a jam on this one, didn't I?" He likes Pereira.

"No, you didn't." Pereira's stare is intense now. "I got you into it."

"All right. Let me answer your question. I think there are lots of people wanting to be deceived in this world. I imagine some in your profession are sincere and others aren't. When my wife booked this appointment I didn't know which group you belonged to."

"What I did before, when we were quiet, was to take in your aura. I first noticed I could do that when I was a boy in Brazil."

"I see."

"Everything is made up of energy. Energy flows freely or energy is blocked. And depending on which it is, your life force is empowered or inhibited."

"No tarot cards, then?"

"Not unless you wish. Some people want their cards read, you know. It can be useful."

"So what will you do with me?"

"I would like to hold your hands now."

Grayson studies the back of the seer's fleshy hands, resting on top of his own upturned palms, when the morning sun strikes the glass surface of the table. He has to close his eyes.

Pereira keeps sitting, seemingly in a different realm. Only after a while does he let go of his client's hands and gets up to close the blinds.

"You have known immense tragedy," he says when he returns to the table. "So immense that you've still not recovered."

Grayson immediately thinks that Samantha must have said something, then remembers that his wife didn't even book the meetings. Maybe Louise Bernstein then.

"You've had a series of shocks, the first of which was a long time ago. In your youth maybe. Involving a parent."

Grayson is stunned. Even if Louise has said something about his accident, she could never have known about this!

Images of his father force themselves on Grayson. Stern and unrelenting, cursing him for getting involved with a girl so far below his station—he, the heir to the car dealership! Telling him to leave and never come back. There are fragments of phone conversations with his distraught mother during the years that follow, parts of the tapestry of gloom that has become her life. Dad turning abusive and insulting, losing customers and staff; Dad getting drunk and smashing things; Dad being taken away to the institution; Dad returning, his spirit smashed and his body dependent on medication and ever larger quantities of root beer and donuts.

Then Grayson feels Marlene's presence. Marlene whose working-class family his father despised so much and whose pull Grayson could not resist. She's near him now and his desire to be with her grows so strong he wants to leave everything for her. The boys, too, but they're less important. Marlene's the one, his Marlene. God, how could he ever have lost her!

"I can't tell which parent you have a problem with," Pereira continues, "but it's unresolved. You never overcame it. Even drew strength from it for a while. The energy it unleashed helped you achieve great success."

No, Marlene's the one who gave him the strength, that's who. Without her, he would never have made it to the top.

"I see tall buildings. And you in position of power. At a young age." Pereira pauses between each of these statements. "And you're married, with a family. There's a large house."

The family, stability. All Marlene's creations. She built a construct of dignity and self-respect his father could never have dreamed of. Majestic, his Marlene. Proving Dad so wrong and rewarding him, Jack, for his decision each day.

"But there are clouds gathering above the house".

Grayson looks up at Pereira and notices his eyes are completely unfocused.

"I'm not sure what the problem is. There's harmony. But something else, too, deep inside you."

"Self-satisfaction," Grayson says harshly and Pereira's head tilts slightly. "Smug self-satisfaction. Conceit."

"That must be it," Pereira passively says, his gaze steadying.

"It was a time of great success for me. I thought nothing could ever go wrong."

"But it did." Pereira gets up and walks to the window. He parts two slats of the blind, briefly looks through them and lets them snap together again. "You've lost your family," he says, as if to himself.

"Yes." Grayson suddenly feels exhausted.

"When I held your hands I felt the cause was physical. An accident maybe."

Grayson sees the gunman raising the pistol, hears the explosion and feels his legs give out under him. He moans and looks up at Pereira, who still stands against the window.

"You are a courageous man, Mr. Grayson."

Grayson fights to keep his emotions in check. "Why are you saying that?"

"You are here. You see yourself the way you are. You have the strength to succeed."

"How do you define success?"

"You've stared death in the face and lost what mattered to you most. And you've come back."

"I have days when I'm in control and others when I feel I'm staring down at yet another abyss." Tears run down Grayson's cheeks.

Pereira looks on for a long moment. "When you talk about being in control I feel a blockage."

Grayson waits for more, then realizes the seer waits for him to respond. "I did have an accident. I was near death and parts of my body haven't fully recovered. And every now and then my brain acts up. I get seizures."

"And you're trying to control the pain?"

"Yes. And sometimes I manage to stop a seizure."

"How do you do it?"

"I concentrate on breathing when I feel it coming. And I do different meditation exercises to prevent it."

Pereira says, "I see. Intellectually at least. But I have a sense that your energy gets blocked by it."

"By breathing? Meditation?"

"By your urge to control. It's something to consider."

Grayson shrugs dismissively.

Pereira continues. "Another thing that comes through strongly. You are struggling with a big decision."

"I guess you know what I'm battling."

"I see things and sometimes they're accurate." Pereira pauses. "Part of it is your wife, isn't it?"

"I don't know what's right." Grayson looks up expectantly.

The seer lifts his hands to his chest, then opens them toward Grayson. "I'm sorry I can't give you advice," he gently says. "Only your heart can tell you what is right and necessary. But there's more than your wife. I feel you have a lot more to deal with. Things going back a long time."

"I know that's true."

"Things from your other lives."

"What, previous incarnations?"

"Perhaps that too. But I meant it figuratively, in terms of dividing our lifespan into episodes. People who've nearly lost their lives and had to start over tend to do that. Immigrants do it too. They often treat life back home as different from their new existence. And sometimes it happens with people who are divorced." He adds playfully, "Oh, my life with Mary—that was another lifetime."

"I guess I have at least two previous lives to think about."

"I already touched on your childhood. There's a lot there."

Grayson exhales deeply and then gets up, holding out his hand. "You zoom right in on things, Mr. Pereira. You're giving me a lot to think about."

Later that day Grayson drives back. He's alone.

Samantha wanted to be dropped off at the beauty studio again, where she checked in for a two-day treatment before coming back by plane.

When saying goodbye at the hotel she thanked him for coming with her, asking him whether seeing Abelard, as she now called him, hadn't been worth every penny. She brought up their dinner conversation too, saying she just couldn't make sense of it. Grayson put on his good face but felt devastated. And now, as he drives on, he tries to understand why.

The sun has made a retreat and by the time he approaches Vail

Pass heavy wet snowflakes muck up his windshield. They make it difficult to drive. Every five minutes or so his wipers succumb to the onslaught of snow and he has to stop to free them. At the rate he's going it will take him at least four more hours to get back to Aspen, but he doesn't mind. More than most people he's had the opportunity to study time. He knows it can manifest itself fleetingly, steal fragment after fragment from him and leave him without recollection of the individual moments that made it up. Or it can punish him agonizingly, enhance every minute of a bad day, amplify each particle of a negative experience.

Once more, Grayson thinks of his time with Samantha and realizes that they haven't spoken about anything of substance for years. He wonders whether they ever did.

Yes, there was the journey from terror to stability they shared and the bliss of being in Hendrick's presence. That was special, he reasons—something he will always treasure. It fused them into one, and that one prevailed in a hostile world.

It must have been later, when their individual selves were reborn, that their relationship started to deteriorate. And Grayson can't believe how long ago that was. Deteriorating is not a good word, he figures, observing the build-up of flakes on the glass in front of him. Melting may be a better choice. That's probably what happened—their relationship melted, like the snow that accumulates through winter dissolves each spring. Neither pleasantly nor unpleasantly, and for no one to witness. You'll know when there's less of it, but you can't see its disintegration. Yet one day, undeniably, it's gone. When, for Jack and Samantha, was that day?

Grayson understands that he needs to find love once more, the kind of love he'd shared with Marlene eons ago. And as he dwells on that realization his mind turns to Ros. He feels a deep long-ing but finds himself wondering what he'd say to her. He's critical of Samantha because he can't talk to her about anything beyond spas and seers and the social set. Yet when with Ros, who's inter-ested in him and sensitive to his problems—what is he willing to talk about? She asks about his father and he backs off. She wants to know more about his sons, but he feels he can't handle it. Yet there's no better listener than Ros. Being his friend isn't easy.

By the time Grayson reaches the stark plateau near Eagle, the snow relents and hues of grey and blue dominate. The desolate landscape and the big sky inspire melancholy. But minutes later, as the first rays of sun break through, the sorrow Grayson feels gives way to tenderness. As he looks at the occasional trailer home or farmhouse near the highway, he understands why it is that people love this place. Like everything, it contains beauty. You just have to bother looking.

He wonders how he can make his own life a place of beauty again and that sends him on an hours' journey of philosophical inquiry. Who am I, is his first question and he knows he does not have an answer. Years of therapy have taught him that he must live in the now, but he sees that he's been drifting from moment to moment rather than dwelling in any one of them. He hasn't worked for years, hasn't challenged himself except with medi-tation and exercise. He's viewed his nightmares and occasional seizures as challenge enough. To the exclusion of all else, he's focused on reducing his pain.

What else could he do, if he wanted to change? The first thought says that his options are limited. Haven't his lawyers told him he can't take another job without losing his pension and the payments from his insurance company?

Then, a breakthrough. He exposes the story he's just made up for what it is: a convenient justification for staying in his rut. Who says he needs to go back to work? Look at Ros. She excels at her photography, attends physics lectures, sketches and reads—apart from running her coffee shop. Grayson sees what's happened, can't believe he hasn't caught on to it before. He's allowed himself to get stuck in hollow routine, just like Samantha.

In Glenwood Springs his tank is down to a quarter. He stops at a Diamond station, walks around the back of his car to where the tank is and turns to the pump. When he holds the nozzle he stops to look around as if to make sure that the black van with its engine running isn't parked nearby. The pump starts to hum and Grayson braces himself for the smell of gasoline. But this time it doesn't bother him.

THE BLOWN-UP PROOF ROS IS working on shows a stand of aspens catching the morning light. It's part of a series of native trees in summer: lush cottonwoods, struggling scrub oaks, spruce bursting with cones, fat twisted pinions. And three different shots of aspens.

When everything looks right, she'll get the studio to pull twenty images of each image and talk to the gallery. Maybe they'll sell them individually, maybe as a numbered edition. She'll have to remember to order an extra set as a gift for Les Bernstein. She grabs her pen and writes herself a note.

Then she turns back to the photograph. Ironically, the most difficult part has turned out perfect: the silvery highlights make the aspen leaves look as though they're actually quaking in the breeze. What Ros isn't happy about is the shade of green.

Green, she thinks. The most difficult color. She closes her eyes, trying to recall what the trees looked like when she photographed them the previous summer. But instead, scenes from impressionist paintings intrude. How well those guys understood color! One day she'll have to visit France and check out the places where they painted: Arles and Saint Rémy and the gardens at Giverny. Not this year though. Too many things going on, Grayson being one of them.

She feels close to him, especially since their talk last night. He told her about his meeting with the seer and how the need to be with Marlene and his sons had overcome him. She felt with him then, wanting nothing more than for him to be reunited with them. Yet Ros felt relief when Grayson mentioned that Marlene was happily remarried. She didn't like that about herself.

Grayson also talked about Samantha: her childlike innocence and her belief that the world was a good place. Given her fragile state when they met, that deeply impressed him.

Still, when Ros considers everything she now knows about Samantha, she finds it hard to understand Grayson's loyalty. But she admires him for it and perhaps that's why she feels drawn to him. He's engaged in a monumental struggle and he's proceeding with courage and honesty.

She thinks of how he started their dinner conversation last night. "Ros, I know it's hard to be my friend." He explained how he'd been driving along thinking about how much he wanted to talk to her, only to realize how often he pulled back. "That must be difficult for you. Sharing the pain, but not the rewards." She lets her mind loop through these words several times.

"It can be tough. But what are your rewards, Grayson?" she remembers asking.

"Just getting it out. Allowing it to rise to my consciousness."

"That helps?"

"Yes, it does. Not always initially though."

"Explain that."

"Sometimes I feel self-pity."

"About why all this stuff is happening to you and not someone else?"

"Yes, about that too."

"And what else?"

"The fact that my assumption is wrong. It's not just happening to me." Ros let him continue.

"It first occurred to me when I was at the hospital. Here I was, wallowing in self-pity for being in a wheelchair while down the hall there was a girl that had been born without a face. A decade of operations ahead, now that her head was fully grown."

Ros reached out her hand, placing it on Grayson's. His speech had slowed, his voice sounded forced.

"I watched a lot of TV, especially at night time. What else was I going to do with myself? The mess in Rwanda was front and centre…1994. A million Tutsis killed, massacred limb by limb by former neighbors wielding machetes. I got into the details, read editorials and backgrounders—I couldn't believe the big powers let that happen. There was a Canadian general, the guy in charge of the UN forces at the time, who thought he could stop it. So he asked for something like ten armoured troop carriers and a couple of transport planes, stuff that was rusting away in nearby Uganda. And the big powers wouldn't give it to him."

"I heard about that."

"You know, I used to think Canada and the US were great nations and the UN an ideal worth supporting. No more. I sympathize with the 60s kids who burned their flags."

"You're bitter, Grayson."

"Bitter, angry—whatever you want to call it. The point I was trying to make is this: it's not just happening to me."

Ros considers. "You're being unfair to yourself. Yes, there are others who suffer immensely, and humans keep doing what they've always done to each other. But that doesn't diminish your own ordeal."

"No, but it brings it into perspective. Look, I feel sorry for myself a lot. But in my more lucid moments I realize others suffer a far worse existence."

"And both your problems and those of others fill you with anger."

"Exactly. I'm getting better at controlling it, but it doesn't always work."

She felt like telling him he should let go, she'd be there for him. But instead, she allowed the conversation to lose itself in inconsequential details. Perhaps that was better.

At her desktop computer Ros experiments with different hues of green. She suspects she needs to add more yellow to the mix, but which one? On the screen in front of her are yellows named after metals like cadmium, nickel, titanium and vanadium. There are iridescent yellows and lemony ones. And finally, ones with names like Hansa and Azo and Permanent.

To Ros, the swatches of color seem like the life choices available to her. Whichever one she chooses, it's certain to irreversibly alter what's there now—perhaps improve it and perhaps blemish or even spoil it. She likes the sound of that last hue the best: permanent.

Ros knows she needs to wait. If she gets too involved with Grayson now, she'll have to let down her guard completely. The leaden weight of her vulnerability settles on her heart as she contemplates that thought. She needs to feel certain—certain that Grayson is what she wants and certain that Grayson is as committed as she is.

A few days ago, on the bridge, she made up her mind not to

be more than his friend. That was a good decision. There are too many unresolved issues in Grayson's life for him to start a relationship. He might not leave Samantha at all or walk out and later change his mind.

Yet despite such misgivings she feels the siren song of her emotions pull her closer to Grayson. It's as though she's standing in the ocean, her head above water and her body intent on moving toward shore, but her legs being pulled into the deep. She's afraid, but part of her wants to surrender to the invisible current and test the unknown.

Ros finds herself sitting at the window looking up at the mountain, without any recollection of walking out onto her deck. Grayson, she thinks. Grayson, it's you who's doing this to me. Her lips open to a deep sigh. She wonders if she's only contemplating falling in love or whether it's already happened.

Ros returns to her computer and opens the file for her aspen image. She zooms in on a particularly lush patch of green and keeps enlarging it until the right-hand half of her screen is filled with no more than a fraction of a single leaf. Without much thought she changes the color, adding one part iridescent yellow and two parts permanent yellow to the mix. When the green on her screen starts to change Ros is stunned. She hits the print command, energized by anticipation, listening to the mechanical clicks of her machine and then watching the sample emerge. She picks it up and studies it, first sitting at her computer and then standing under the skylight. She can't believe how perfect it is.

4

ROS STANDS OUTSIDE THE THATCHED roof hut they've rented. They've been in Tulum for a week. She's never dreamed of traveling here, thinking Mexico would be similar to Australia. But the textures and colors she sees are more intense and joyful than anything she's ever seen at home. Fire and blood, she thinks, but then her eyes catch the weathered pink stucco and the cracked sky-blue shutters of their hut and she changes her verdict. Fire and blood, yes—but tempered by a flirtatious softness. She's determined to do an edition on Mexico while she's here. Not having brought enough of her tools will make things more difficult, but she'll enjoy the challenge.

Ros is eager to get working. She loved the first few days, but now she's feeling uneasy, the way she gets at home when it's her day off work and she's between projects.

She notices Grayson talking to one of the laborers. She's intrigued, realizing how little she knows about him. Once or twice she's seen Grayson talk to people at the café and on the street—people he knows. She thinks of him as quiet and thoughtful, not outgoing. And yet here he is, engaging a local in conversation.

Grayson looks trim and muscular and his tan makes him look

healthy. Ros smiles. How strange that things have worked out this way.

But have they really worked out? She reminds herself of the uncertainties they'll have to face when they get back, then decides to concentrate on her time here. Grayson seems relaxed and loving toward her, but so far they've stayed away from his past. Ros wonders how long that can last.

She tries to imagine how she would feel in his situation and as she does so, long buried issues of her own float to the surface. She looks out at the Caribbean surf, but her mind takes her to Melbourne's Brighton Beach. Ian is walking away toward the small flat they share, carrying his surfboard as if it were weightless, his sun-darkened oiled body glistening with a million droplets. Next, Ros' mind sees a younger version of herself lying at the beach, her head propped up on her elbows. The sand feels hot against her belly and she wonders when she'll have the courage to tell Ian. Then she watches herself get up and follow him and next they're standing inside their place and she says it. No tears, not much emotion even—it's almost as if someone else spoke the sentence.

Ian looks awkward. He says he'll have to get a job then and marry her, his eyes cast to the ground. And when that's said and he looks up at Ros who's leaning back at the wall feeling numb and worthless, he can't bear it and walks out the door.

Ros remembers the months of self-doubt and loneliness that followed, all compressed into a couple of seconds now, and finally she turns to her last encounter with Ian as she always does, a monochrome clip of Ros entering their bedroom and Ian busy fucking their neighbor's daughter—monochrome because she can't for the life of her remember what color the walls or the rug or the bedspread were. She can't even remember the girl's face. All she sees is a pleading, shamed pair of eyes.

Ros fingers search for the ring as they did then, but there's nothing to pull off any longer. All she feels is skin and knuckle.

Later, as Ros and Grayson indulge in their evening ritual of sharing a drink, she asks him about Hendrick Hegedus.

"What about him?"

"Tell me how you heard of him, why you decided to go to the retreat."

Grayson gets up from his deck chair, walks to the porch railing and looks out to sea. "It was a shot in the dark. Sharon Bailey at the hospital knew about it."

"And you signed up"

"Checked in is a better description."

"Just like that? For several months, Grayson?"

"Strange. Here we are, after absconding to a distant beach in Mexico. And you still call me Grayson."

Ros gets up and joins him at the railing. "Do you want me to call you Jack?"

He reflects. "No. I like it when you call me Grayson. You're the only one who's ever done that, you know. It makes for a nice break. Jack is what people called me in my other life—better not to return there too often."

Ros reads that as a hint, but persists, seeking his eyes. "About the retreat…"

"If I didn't like it, I could always leave, couldn't I? You've got to realize, Ros, I was willing to try anything."

"But you were getting better, weren't you?"

"Only physically."

"I thought you had Sharon Bailey and the meditation classes and all that."

"Things got better at first, yes, but not once I got home."

Ros can tell from Grayson's voice that he's gone to a place where he's all alone. She wants to hold him but senses his rigidity. "We're reaching that point again, aren't we?" she whispers. "I'm pushing you too hard."

"Sometimes you don't know when to push."

Ros is on the verge of asking how she's supposed to know when and how much, but then decides to hold back. Instead, she walks back to the table inside the hut, picks up her camera and lifts it. Through the lens she can see Grayson facing out to the darkening ocean, his broad back like a slab of concrete. She clicks.

The next morning is a good one. The sun is still sitting low on the horizon and schools of pelicans skim the surf. Every now and then the birds veer off to the beach and pass a few feet above them. Ros and Grayson are resting on their elbows, craning their necks to observe the spectacle of flight.

"You asked about Hendrick yesterday," Grayson starts.

"Are you sure you want to go back there?"

"I think so. I just have to find the right times."

For an instant, Grayson's comment irks Ros, making her wonder why he always gets to set the terms. Then she feels badly and lets her hand search for his. She knows it's hard for him.

"I went to Hendrick because I completely crashed."

"After you got back home?"

"Yes."

"What happened?"

"I've thought about it a lot. I guess rehab, meditation and doctors checking on me were a routine. Going back was a shock."

"But you must have been eager to get home."

"It wasn't the home I left." Grayson's voice is strained. "In hospital I started from nothing and I could progress. When they let me go I'd come a long way. But once I got home my point of reference changed completely. Everything reminded me how far I'd slipped backward."

"You left healthy and returned in a wheelchair."

"I left being the provider and now I was back as a dependent. And then Marlene and the boys. Always nice, always available to help. And acting as though I'd always been a fucking cripple."

Ros wants to ask what else they should have done but decides to just listen.

"There were other pressures, too. Related to my career, my self-image. The story of how I saw myself, how I felt others saw me—all that had to be rewritten. Every connection with life or people, every association in my brain had to be rethought. Later came the sex thing. I couldn't do it anymore, I was paralyzed. Which meant I thought about it all the time. Each time I saw Marlene..." Grayson lets himself fall back onto the sand and frowns at the brightening sky above him, his eyes out of focus.

He tries again. "Each time I saw Marlene I knew I was a bit closer to losing her, frustrated that I could not satisfy myself and even more upset that she had to be without it. Then I started looking at other women, thinking that someone out there might stimulate me enough to get me going again. Hospital workers, women in the elevator, at the coffee place Marlene used to take me in my wheelchair."

Grayson moves forward onto his knees and his hands start scooping up sand and letting it sift through his fingers. "I lost sight of the progress I'd made in hospital. It seemed so irrelevant. I started to think I'd have to stay in the wheelchair forever. My anger came back."

"What about meditating?"

"I tried that. Over and over. But all I could find was self-pity and anger. It's interesting, when I started meditating at the hospital, I visualized the energy entering me as a blue light. I'm not sure where that came from; maybe I read it somewhere and it worked. But it was the most vivid blue I could imagine. And it had a healing effect on me. Now, my breath was blackness. Blackness that entered and blackness that left when I exhaled."

"God."

"I tried to understand what was happening. Grasp it intellectually. It felt like dense black ink engulfing me. At first I fought it, but then my body and mind became eager to soak it up. We no longer just coexisted but it became part of me. I fed it and it fed me." Grayson lets his shoulders and head fall back on the sand and exhales loudly. "You know what the worst thing is when you're dependent?"

Ros waits for an answer, but none comes. "What?" she asks.

"You're like a fucking missile. You're so angry and frustrated you destroy everything in your path. And here's the clincher: the only people in your path are the ones who care for you."

"What do you mean?"

"Marlene. Good old Marlene. Carting me around, feeding me, changing my incontinence pads. And what did I do? Hurt her whenever I could. I made her pay for my misery."

"Why?"

"Because she was the only one who was there, you see?" His voice is starting to choke. "She and the boys. They were there for me and I abused them, day after miserable day. On the other hand we had this part-time nurse, pretty young Celia. I could have taken it out on her too, but I didn't. In fact my behaviour was at its best when she was around. I had to have one person who only saw me at my best."

"Oh, Grayson."

"It got worse. Celia started to feel so goddamn sorry for me she fell in love. One day Marlene opens the door coming in with Oliver, the older boy, and here I am in my wheelchair, with the nurse sucking my cock, trying to find some life signs."

Ros' hand reaches for Grayson, then hesitates in mid air.

"That was a year after the accident—almost to the day," Grayson says, as though such trivia lessened the weight of his words or helped him cope with his pain. Then he pushes himself up and starts walking toward the ocean. After a few steps he starts to run, his limp more noticeable than usual, and once he's in knee-deep surf, he starts to frantically splash himself.

He stays in the water for a long time.

There are pelicans and sandpipers, crabs and iguanas here to sketch, but Ros' mind keeps returning to dragon flies and damsel-flies. God knows why.

She adds a few strokes to the thorax of the male, finishes the huge compound eyes that make up most of his head, and finally turns to the tail. She needs it curved so that the clasping organ at its end can hold the female behind her neck.

The bodies on Ros' pad are pencil-gray but she sees them in

metallic green, flitting across the water at breathtaking speed even as they're joined together. ZYGOPTERA—ENALLAGMA ASPERSUM, she scrawls at the bottom of the page.

"What are they?" asks Grayson, having watched and assuming she's finished.

"Guess."

"Damselflies, I think."

"Yes, that's what zygoptera means. But what species?"

Grayson looks closer. "I can't tell."

"It's tough to tell them apart. These are azure bluets."

"You should describe that in English. 'Azure bluets mating' would be better than the Latin stuff."

"But they're not mating. At least not yet."

"Then why is he holding her like that?"

"Hoping." Ros laughs.

"Ah, foreplay. I didn't think animals did much of that."

"You'd be surprised."

"And what happens next?"

"She's got to turn her tail upward so that it reaches right under his abdomen. That's where his sperm is." Ros gestures at her pad. "Like this."

They're sitting on the steps of their porch, Ros adding to the background of her sketch, Grayson studying the breaking surf.

"This is so therapeutic," he says after a while.

"Isn't it? I'm glad I have the sketchbook here, though. I'm not used to doing nothing."

"Maybe this is the perfect chance to try. I don't think I've ever seen you do nothing."

"Don't worry about me. I'll cope."

"You know, Ros, this wouldn't be a bad time for you to learn to meditate."

Ros doesn't know why, but she bristles at the thought. "I'm doing just fine, thanks."

"Gee, that doesn't sound very receptive."

"Like I said, Grayson, I'm fine." Her contentment of a few seconds ago is gone and she wonders why that is. She knows she's the one who's asked Grayson about meditation half a dozen times.

"I just brought it up because…"

"I know. But let's just leave it, okay?"

"Okay. I hear you, but I don't understand."

"God, what's there to understand? I'm not interested, that's all. I'm doing just fine." She knows she sounds hysterical now.

"All right, whatever." Grayson gets up. "I'm going to walk down the beach." He starts moving.

Ros pushes herself up too. "No, it's not whatever," she shouts. "You don't get to control everything. I can decide what's right for me, for God's sake!"

Grayson turns back. He becomes aware that his head is pounding. "It's better if I walk now. By myself."

Ros lowers her eyes onto the white sand and says, "Go then," and watches Grayson awkwardly walk off, a dozen sandpipers scattering at his approach.

Her thoughts are chaotic and she feels like crying but dismisses the urge as ridiculous. She needs to calm herself. It takes Ros a while to sort out why she's here and what just happened, but when she understands she gets up and runs.

Once she's caught up with Grayson she stands opposite him for a long moment, studying his eyes. They reveal nothing in their impenetrable blueness, like oceans of vast depth and soft-ness, whose surface appears harsh and unbending in the relentless breeze. Ros reaches up for his face and holds it before she kisses him gently. His lips taste salty. They kiss again, longer and deeper each time, and when they kneel at the edge of the ocean together she feels his hardness against her and that makes her desire him even more.

On the way back to their hut Grayson stops to pick a hibiscus flower and puts it in her hair.

ROS HEARS THE BED CREAK and turns her head so she can see into the hut. Grayson is sitting on the edge, smiling at her. She smiles back, but as she does she feels anxiety rise in her.

Ros' problem is this: she and Grayson are only here for a few more days. She worries, asks herself questions she can't answer. What if he goes back to Samantha? And if he doesn't, what kind of a life will they have together?

During the three weeks they've been here Ros and Grayson have talked mostly about the past: Marlene and Hendrick and Sharon Bailey, and later her father and Ian. But now the focus is turning to the future. Uncertainty and doubt dominate her thoughts of what will be next week and next month. They need to talk about where and how they'll live.

Taking off in such a hurry was a mistake. Less than a month ago Ros vowed not to get involved without Grayson first leaving Samantha and living by himself for a while. But then, one night he came to pick her up at the café and she changed all that.

Ros sighs as she relives the scene. There she is, leaning against the filing cabinet in her small office, fumbling with Grayson's shirt buttons and intently watching his eyes as they change from surprise to wonderment and then transform again, to an expression she's seen a few times since and come to treasure. How determined she was to become Grayson's lover that night, her desire blotting out all reason and suppressing even the fear of making herself vulnerable.

The images playing in her mind bring on new emotions. Now she feels guilt about what she's done, wondering if she could ever face Samantha and what she'd say to her. And regret about putting Grayson into this situation too. She's made a mess of things.

When Ros hears Grayson cough, she turns her eyes back to him and sees that he's still sitting on the edge of the bed.

"A penny for your thoughts," he says.

"Do you really want to know, Grayson?"

"Sure."

"Then come on out. We'll walk. Walking is curative."

"Sounds serious," Grayson says, tilting his head curiously.

She takes his hand and they start strolling toward the water. The sun is high, the sand hard to look at.

"I'm thinking of what will be when we return, Grayson. Not without anxiety."

"I know."

"We could have done this differently." She seeks his eyes.

"Maybe, Ros. But we didn't."

"So what do we do?"

"We return and see."

"We return where, Grayson? Have you given that any thought?"

"Are you worried about Samantha?"

"Yes, Samantha's on my mind a lot. I feel terrible about going behind her back. I'm apprehensive."

"About what she might do?"

"That too, but also about what you might do."

"I see."

"Shouldn't I be, Grayson?"

For a moment he considers. Then he stops, reaches around Ros' shoulders and draws her to him. "That depends, Ros."

"On what?"

"On whether you want to be with me." Grayson waits for an answer but there is none. He studies her face, its pleasantly tanned skin almost the same shade as the strands of hair dancing in the breeze. His gaze comes to rest on her hazel eyes, ablaze now with something he can't read but which bids him to say more.

He feels Ros take hold of his hands and that emboldens him. "I'm a sick man. Bad dreams wake me up at night and my leg's a mess." His voice is scratchy. "And you know all about my damaged brain, Ros." As he says this he looks out at the vastness of the sea and the line far away where water and sky meet.

"I can accept it," Ros whispers.

Grayson's eyes return to hers and the fire is still there. "And I'm ten years older."

"I take that too, old man."

"Then there's only one option. We must give it a try, the two of us."

It's what Ros needs to hear.

When first experimenting with doing nothing for half an hour each day, Ros wondered how she'd fit it into her day once she got busy again, in Aspen. Now such thoughts are gone. Already it's become a practice she won't want to do without.

Grayson keeps offering to share his insights into meditation, but Ros is determined not to call it that. Instead, she refers to her ritual as her afternoon contemplation. That way there is no pressure to adhere to any rules. All Ros does during her quiet time is sit and absorb what unfolds before and around her. Sometimes her eyes are open, in a relaxed and often unfocused way, and sometimes they're closed as she takes in whatever sounds arise or feels the ocean breeze caress her body.

Sometimes she pays attention to her breathing, too, allowing the air to enter through her nostrils and feeling her abdomen gradually expanding. Once or twice she's even wondered whether the energy of the breath isn't actually entering through her skull, just as it leaves through the palms of her hands and the soles of her feet. She knows she'll share that with Grayson when the time is right.

Now Ros becomes aware of a distant voice—a girl singing. With her eyes still closed, she starts listening attentively, then gives the voice her full attention. She contemplates its purity and youth and contrasts it to the sound of the surf. Then she hears others—ten, perhaps twenty playing children, their voices seemingly competing for dominance. And then, as Ros opens herself completely, the many voices unexpectedly become one and she recognizes the unlimited potential of this one voice and knows it must be the vibration of the universe itself—it and the ancient ocean whose swelling surf now sings along too.

Ros is reluctant to allow her eyes to open again and when she does, it takes a while to adjust to the glassy brightness of the simmering sand that stretches before her.

GRAYSON IS ILL AT EASE. The house feels even emptier than usual. There are none of the tell-tale signs of Samantha's presence that once livened up the vast rooms. No gloves and scarves on the hall-way bench and no pantyhose carelessly thrown on the bathroom floor. The clutter on the kitchen table is gone.

He half expected that Samantha would be gone and now he knows. Grayson sees the envelope, stark white against the black granite of the cooking counter, the letters J-A-C-K written in Samantha's girlish hand, both innocent and foreboding. Then he sees the lavender sprig lying next to it. He's not sure whether it was left by design. Grayson picks it up but it's so dry it crumbles between his fingers. He feels clumsy and sad.

He takes Samantha's envelope, looks at it for several seconds, then puts it down again, too agitated to read it now.

Later, when he returns to the kitchen, he holds a list of the things he'll need to move. Clothes, ski equipment and bike, old photo albums and videotapes, two or three dozen books, his laptop and files—things that are of no use to Samantha. He remembers his bathroom stuff and adds it to the list: toothbrush, shaving kit, all that.

The orchids are on his mind too. Two of the plants look

unhappy, their bottom leaves having turned a sickly shade of olive. But all the others, thanks to Ros' coffee-shop assistant Anna, are in fine shape. He knows how much Samantha likes them, but would she be able to do justice to them?

Grayson decides to leave them off his list for now, then reviews his scribbles and is relieved there's so little. Two trips in his Highlander should do it.

When he comes to the top of Smuggler, Grayson is panting. He's out of shape. Making love and sitting at the beach did that.

He stands for a while, getting his breath under control. He can see the prominent skylights of his house far below him and then looks to the other side of town, trying to spot Ros' place. All he can make out is a hodgepodge of roofs tightly pressed together. Where exactly Ros lives is impossible to say. Behind the small houses rises Aspen Mountain, the gondolas hanging immobile and the skiers gone. A patchwork of dirt and bits of left-over snow interspersed with stands of bluish-green conifers and leafless aspens make up the mountainside.

Grayson looks for a place to sit and sees a fallen tree a bit further up the path. He walks up to it, grabs his water bottle and drinks. Then he settles down, opens the zipper of his waist pack and pulls out Samantha's yet unopened envelope.

When he holds the single sheet of paper he's surprised there isn't more. How much she must have wanted to say and couldn't express when they had their talk. And now only this. He feels at once cheated and relieved.

His gaze returns to his house and he thinks of the evening when he told her. He'd walked up to the front door, the flames of his guilt pushing him to go in, but he ended up standing outside for a long time watching black clouds swell up in front of an intensely blue sky. Next, there was lighting, followed by thunderclaps so deafening he felt compelled to cover his ears. Later, freezing rain flogged his face. But he stayed, wet and miserable, until the sky calmed, and only then did he go in and talk to Samantha.

Grayson lowers his eyes to the letter. 'Dear Jack,' it starts. He's expected 'Jack!' or maybe 'Jack, you bastard!' He knows he'll feel even guiltier now.

Dear Jack,

I am trying not to be resentful and I'm not sure I can do it. If anything can help me cope it's the ashram I've wanted to go to for some time. I'm not sure if they have a waiting list or schedule or if you just show up and check in. So I'm just flying to Bangalore to see where it leads. I may even find one of my friends there, and if not I'm sure I'll make new ones.

What hurts me most is that you betrayed me with the coffee shop woman, probably for all these years. You're saying this isn't true, but I can't get myself to believe it. I will find it hard to ever trust you again, although that may be irrelevant.

I have only two wishes and, no, I haven't gone to see a lawyer. You were right about that. All it would do is create anger and resentment, and God knows you and I have had enough of that for a few lifetimes. Besides, between the money you brought and what you're still receiving from the insurance, and what I got from my mother's estate, we'll both be set—no matter how we split things.

Jack, my first wish is that you leave me the house. I know you don't care about it, but I do. I love that house and I'll finally build the gym you always opposed. The other thing is more difficult. I feel this is all so embarrassing that I would like you to leave the valley. If you must be in this part of the country, go to Santa Fe or Boulder or Telluride. I don't think I could bear the humiliation of having you and your friend living in the same town.

I don't know when I'll be back. Probably not for several weeks. When I come, I hope you will have moved your things out. Take whatever you want. At some point we will have to meet and finalize the details of our separation. I can't imagine anything more hurtful right now, but I will find the strength.

I find it hard not to resent what you have done, Jack, especially betraying me, but I wish you well.

Sam

It takes Grayson less than two minutes to read. But he sits there a long time, at the side of the path, chilled to the bone by the mountain breeze, but not noticing.

ROS CAN READ HIS SADNESS as soon as he walks in. And he seems more distant, even after she joins him at the table. Come to think of it, his visit here at the café feels odd, now that they are together.

Grayson expresses her thoughts. "It's strange for you to bring me cappuccino now," he says.

She laughs. "For me too. I'm used to be sitting at the beach waiting for you to bring me my Margarita."

Grayson glances at her seriously. "We could do that all the time."

"What do you mean?"

"Samantha wants me out of the valley."

"You say that so solemnly, Grayson. You must have expected it."

He looks up to her. "It's strange, but I haven't. Getting out of the house, yes. But moving away isn't something I've given much thought to."

"What's here, anyway?" Ros says simply.

"Not much for me except the great outdoors. I was thinking about you, Ros."

Ros says, "I can be anywhere, Grayson," then thinks about her art and Bernstein's restaurant and the job she likes. "As long as we can be together."

"There's Mexico. A never-ending stream of Margaritas just the way you like them. And fifty feet from us the ocean."

"No. I'd be bored stiff. That doesn't mean I couldn't take ten days of it every winter."

"Samantha's suggestions aren't bad. She thinks we may like Boulder or Telluride. Or Santa Fe."

Ros reaches for his hands. "How did it go?"

"She wasn't there."

"She's gone away?"

"Gone to India for a while. She left a letter, though." Grayson looks distraught. "A nice, honest letter. It makes me feel like a jerk."

Ros gets up to serve the customer who's just walked in. She mechanically takes the order, fills the scoop with coffee and inserts it into the machine. The she pressed a button.

This is where it started, she thinks. Where we first made love, right over there in my office, after I locked up. And now Samantha is in India.

The hiss of the espresso machine interrupts her thoughts. When she looks up she realizes that Grayson has been watching her. He's leaning back in his chair, slightly rocking it. His arms are folded. Ros tries to guess what he's thinking.

Mid-May brings the season's last snowstorm. Nearly two feet of powder have fallen, spoiling the blossoms on the crab apple trees that line the town's streets and burying budding gardens. The plows can be heard one last time, rumbling when their blades plane on the white surface and screeching in agony when they probe too deep and hit concrete. By afternoon the clouds have parted and the fresh snow lays heavy, the crystals lazily expanding in the spring weather, not aware how harsh the night will be.

Ros' life has changed. Grayson now waits for her when she gets home and sometimes he cooks dinner. And he stays the nights. In the morning, Ros no longer rushes to the café to open up; she relies on Anna to do that. Instead she stays in bed longer, savoring Grayson's closeness. This morning is no different. It's nearly ten when she gets going.

As Ros walks through her front door the snow-covered meadow outside blinds her. She adjusts her eyes and takes in what looks like a massive sequined blanket. Then she walks closer and studies the crystals on top, sucked dry of all moisture, an array of tiny spears and splinters of which each has a part that reflects the morning sun and a shadow side that gleams blue. A few birds have come out of hiding. They're darting around chaotically, perplexed by the mass of snow and distraught about the disappearance of their food sources.

Ros reflects on the pictures she could shoot. She used to live for scenes like these, but now she just shrugs. There's been no time for her art and she accepts it. As long as she's alive and aware, there will always be another great shot. What matters now is her relationship with Grayson and the decisions they'll have to make.

She needs to talk to Les Bernstein before long. Even though she hopes he'll keep her photographs at his restaurant, and maybe accept others to replace the ones that sell, she knows the conversation will be awkward. He'll ask about her and Grayson. And if he doesn't it'll be worse.

And where will they go? She doesn't think the idea of moving elsewhere bothers her, but what if they can't agree on a place or if one of them doesn't like it when they get there? Ros has reason to worry; she senses that Grayson has a hard time deciding. He's told her several times that it's she who needs to make a clear choice, but each time she mentions a place where she could live Grayson stalls. A few times their discussions have threatened to become arguments, but in the end she's always pulled back, telling him he should take his time.

Ros reminds herself that this is the only friction point in their relationship. Most evenings when Grayson comes to her place, all goes well. They go for walks, see movies and read to each other. And they make love a lot.

When she lies with him at night she dreams of their new life. She's always projected her sensuality into her art, but now she feels a desire to make life itself sensual. She's decided to spoil Grayson, wherever it's going to be. She'll learn more about food and wines and place fresh flowers on the table. And she'll make herself more attractive, too. She'll become irresistible to him.

THE EXPANSES OF DIRT WHICH were bared by the receding snow pack have turned into juicy meadow. The grass is thick and of a green so intense that it seems imaginary. And in between the grass there are bunches of wildflowers, every bit as unreal, showing from afar as passionate specks of red, yellow and blue.

Grayson dreamily looks at the hillside outside his office. He takes the envelope off his desk and tears it open; it contains a postcard and a single sheet of paper, neatly folded.

The card looks as illusory as the meadow at which he's been gazing. It shows a farmer holding on to a plow, which is being pulled by a pair of oxen. Behind the plowing team are a vast field and a replete sun about to sink into the earth. All in different hues of brown. The farmer's face bronze and his flowing robe ochre. The plow blade burnt umber and the yawning furrow it's left in the soil even darker. The field behind a sea of raw sienna. Even the sun is brown: a rusted platter, radiating decay and renewal at the same time.

She's always uprooting herself, Grayson thinks. She's very good at that, Samantha. I'm sitting here, still not sure what will be next, and she's in India.

Next, he unfolds the piece of paper and, for a few moments,

lets his unfocused eyes rest on the tiny, pencilled scrawls. He wonders whether he would have left Samantha if it weren't for Ros.

And then he starts to read.

Dear Jack.

I'm at the Shimsha Krishna ashram, approx. 50 mi. from Bangalore, near a town called Maddur. His Holiness (that's what we call him— his real name is Swami Sivananda and several names behind that!) is out of this world. So serene and composed! I keep re-learning all kinds of things I forgot, so I'll be here for a while longer.

Jack, I think a lot about our life together. The thing with Ros still bothers me, but I've forgiven you. I hold your picture deep in my heart and I only feel good things. Have you given some thought to where you could move? I hope you'll respect my wish. I need to think about my future, too. I think I'm off to a good start.

May your inner light shine strongly!

Love, Sam.

PS, Jack: Several Americans here, so I'm never lonely. And Judy Vital is expected to arrive next week. Imagine that!

Grayson puts the postcard down. He hears Samantha say the words that stick: *Have you given some thought to where you could move?* As he's done so many times recently, he asks himself where he and Ros will end up. There are times when he thinks they're meant for each other, and then he convinces himself that she won't put up with him for much longer.

Grayson's feelings change depending on the time of day. On his morning-jog up Smuggler Mountain and during the hours he spends aimlessly puttering at the house, he lets his emotional baggage creep up on him. Thoughts about Samantha and scenes from his years with Marlene and the boys batter him. Occasionally he manages to summon Hegedus' iconic image and draws a semblance of calm from it, but within minutes or even seconds, the discordant notes and images that make up the opera of his life resume their frenetic pace. Worst are the voices of his parents, calling him from somewhere deep and demanding to be heard. Mom's voice timid and panicky, his father's overbearing and taut as a cord ready to snap. He keeps resisting them, but it's getting harder.

Grayson is learning to keep Ros out of it. She's shown him the way, telling him she'd like to change the terms of their relationship. "It's got to do with our conversations," she began on their flight returning from Mexico. "They're becoming one-sided." Her comment was unexpected and badly timed. The seats were uncomfortable and they were sweating profusely, the overhead jet blasting stale, warm air at them. "Grayson, I don't mind discussing your past; it's essential that you come to terms with it and I want to help. But I'd like for us to discuss other things as well." He didn't respond then, but he could see Ros was right. All they ever talked about was his past.

And yet, her request left him bewildered. Only a few weeks ago it was he who had told Samantha there should be more talk between them. What would he have wanted to discuss had Samantha been interested? Grayson had to admit he didn't know. Gradually it dawned on him that he no longer expressed his feelings, except to himself. Perhaps he'd always done that.

So now, when he and Ros are together, he lets her initiate the conversation. She's good at it, too, challenging or gently goading him into exchanges of view, pushing him to relate sentiments or insecurities or passions. And sometimes their evening and night is empty of talk, there just for the love between them and the hope of a future together.

Grayson sits in front of his paper, trying to make sense of what's up in Libya. It looks like the U.S.-led invasion has converted the country from a functioning state on decent terms with its neighbours to one where slavery and human trafficking have become mainstays of the economy.

He's aware of the negativity his habit creates; for days now, he's observed what digesting the news does to him. It tightens him physically. His stomach contracts, his neck stiffens. He's come to believe that his own experience must be that of the collective American psyche, as well. Obsession with news and dread of the news. A fear-based society exploited by an uncaring but highly sophisticated media complex controlled by its corporate masters.

Fuel the public's dread of terrorists, drug lords and illegal immigrants and, bingo, the public ends up in a continuous state of xenophobic hysteria. Occasionally, stoke the fear of deteriorating credit ratings and penniless retirement, too. Or dwell on the prospect of losing what money there is to fraudsters or Wall Street's army of silver-tongued thieves. And let's not forget the annual flu shot and the need to prevent our teeth from turning yellow.

Grayson's bum leg, already tense, starts to throb, even before his mind loops him back to the topic of where he started. The lingering phobia of a mushroom cloud rising over a U.S. city, courtesy of the latest rogue nation, which leads to a whole subset of worries, including fear of what will happen if the would-be aggressors are not taken out first.

Then he notices the obituary: Charlie Kloss, a long-time local. He knows Ros doesn't care about Libya or the anxiety-packed psyche of Greater America, but this he wants to share. He reads it out loud.

Ros listens, says she knew Charlie. "But I don't like his obit, Grayson. They've reduced his life to a bunch of milestones."

"That's all there is in the end. What do you think they'd say of me?"

"Come on, I hope it would be better than this."

Grayson ignores her. "Born in Ontario, Canada. Son of a car dealer and his wife," he started. "Graduated. Got married. Two sons. Joined Continental Group. Youngest executive in the company's history. Tragic accident and partial recovery. Bingo."

"Well, that wouldn't reflect your life, would it?"

"You tell me. Who am I, if not a sequence of milestones? What's wrong with reciting them?"

"What's wrong? For starters, you didn't even list me among your milestones," Ros teases. "But beyond that—it's not reflective of you. It would be soul-less."

"Soul-less?"

"Yes, a you stripped of meaningful content. What about life being a series of decisions? Surely the forks in the road are more important than the milestones. As is the journey between one milestone and another."

"You have a point."

"Milestones have little substance. Think of it, what matters—the years or decades of a marriage or the wedding day?"

Again, Grayson has to agree. He realizes what Ros says has relevance for his own life. "What do you think are the events that really do matter? I mean, how would you write your own obituary, if you'd died yesterday?"

"Well, I'd ask myself what the most important days of my life were. I'd try to express what I felt then and why I felt it."

"And what were those days?"

Ros pondered the question. "Remember, you told me about the seer. How he said some people break their lives up into segments."

"Right."

"Well, I do that. Australia is another life for me. It's the past—no, not just that, it's someone else's past."

"What about later? Important days after Australia?"

"One such time was when you sat with me all night, after my father died. Another when you told me that you'd found me a new apartment. And then there's the hibiscus flower day." Ros' face has lit up.

"The what?"

"When you picked up that hibiscus flower and put it in my hair. In Mexico."

"It was that important?"

"Yes. It was a metaphor, Grayson. Our talks about the past were becoming a bridge between us, and that bridge made tenderness possible. I had seen you gentlemanly before you picked up that flower, but not tender."

"Now, technically that was both a milestone and a fork in the road, right?" Grayson asserts as he gets up, muttering something about going to the toilet.

Inside the bathroom he turns on the tap and just stands

there, watching the water run. The echo of Ros' words fires his emotions. He considers his life since the accident, years without definition. There were milestones, yes. Recovery, his first meditations and the retreat. Meeting Samantha and overcoming adversity together. And then a meaningless flurry of chatter that ended up filling years. Not a milestone, that, but miles of well-paved highway, the scenery pleasant but by no means stimulating. Samantha wasn't able to give him more.

Did he give her what she needed? Grayson shakes his head slowly, unaware of the movement. He places his hands under the tap and welcomes the sobering cold of the water. He doesn't rub his hands—the thought doesn't occur to him. Just holds them, feeling them chill down to the temperature of the icy water.

It couldn't have lasted, he's sure of that now. Samantha, the restless socialite, and he, the recluse. How he hated to go to parties with her! He remembers Samantha steering him around other people's houses, always looking for new connections, the drudgery of small-talk and gossip inescapable.

He turns off the tap, dries his hands and sits down on the toilet, pants on. His mind's eye sees Samantha's postcard, takes in the tiny writing again and rests on the sentence near the bottom: *Have you given some thought to where you could move?*

He's talked about possible places with Ros, but they've agreed not to rush their decision. A few nights ago Ros even questioned the idea of picking a permanent place. How about putting everything into storage and just travel for a year or two? To the Provence perhaps, or Umbria. He mentioned Sicily, the Pyrenees and Patagonia as places he always wanted to see.

On the other side of the wall, Ros' voice is asking if he's all right. Grayson shouts he'll be a minute. Then he leans back and closes his eyes.

He's never done anything like this. Life was always focused: first on family and career, later on rehabilitation. And when he repossessed his body, he concentrated on keeping chaos at bay. He knows he doesn't like change, but he's starting to believe that it's good for him. Ros is good for him!

They're sitting at Ros' small kitchen table, plates pushed aside, enjoying the wine that's left. Grayson reflects on the time he wasn't allowed to drink, when it interfered with his pharmaceutical cocktails. He tells Ros.

"You've been off those meds for a while, haven't you?" she asks.

"I stopped a few years ago. The warnings of side effects got to me."

"But you stayed off alcohol?"

"Samantha and I drank Diet Coke ever since we got together. It became a habit, I guess, like dozens of other things. You are the one who got me back into this deplorable habit, Ros."

She laughs. "Do you regret it?"

"No, I just want to have someone to blame if my liver goes on strike."

They look at each other, grateful they can share humour, and reach for their glasses.

"Ros, about our discussions before—the milestones."

"That got to you, didn't it?"

"Yes, you got me thinking. Milestones aren't the key, I agree, but how do you capture the essence of a life?"

Ros thinks, takes another sip of wine. "What if we asked

people not who they are, but what their best three life experiences were? Most likely, we'd get to hear about little things. Experiences society never learns about. Experiences that really matter, that define them like no milestones can."

"Like Citizen Kane's Rosebud."

"Like that."

It's close to midnight and Grayson still lays awake. It's tight in Ros' bed. A lazy quarter moon dangles in the window near him. It arcs to the left; that means it's descending.

Grayson's arm reaches below his thigh, his fingers massaging the ache that reaches from knee to spine. He tries to do this without waking Ros, whose breathing comforts him. His mind still dwells on their conversation; since going to bed he's been wondering what the little things in his life are. Things that have shaped him as an individual, be they successes or failures. Or things that define him—belongings like Rosebud, or beliefs, obsessions. What are they?

So far, Grayson has thought about his time with Samantha and that keeps leading him to Hegedus. Hendrick has shaped him, of that he can be certain. If anything, he's Hendrick Hegedus' creation.

But what else? Grayson ponders his more distant past and realizes too late that going there is a mistake. For a few moments his recollections are blurry, faint dancers representing years of his life seen through dense fog. Then the figures take shape. First Marlene and soon after it's Marlene and Oliver, and whenever he sees his younger son there is Celia also, kneeling in front of his wheelchair. Soon the thoughts come at him at an alarming rate, one packed inside the other like Russian matryoshka dolls, negativity neatly stored inside their charmingly painted exteriors. His mind is too busy to notice how his body responds: whole muscle groups working in concert to tighten his stomach, neck and throat and mostly his fucked-up leg. But whether he feels it or not is irrelevant, because his overloaded brain has already sent out a caustic message designed to poison all systems. Why me? Why is this happening to me?

There is Grayson in some boardroom, wearing a dark suit, his promotion sparking a flicker of pride. That is gone again in a nanosecond and next he sees himself in jeans and a pastel colored T-shirt, holding a much younger Marlene's hand. The two of them are dwarfed by a massive desk and the enormous figure standing behind it.

Grayson doesn't need to listen to the words to know where he is. He sees the protruding temple veins and the nervous tick just below the left eye and can measure his father's anger by the venomous spittle darting from between his lips.

The weight of Grayson's heart grows, and as he begins to understand density spreads through his body until he feels like a bag of buckshot. What Grayson is grasping is this. The little things he's looking for are in his past; the key to who he is may be hidden in his youth, perhaps even his childhood.

WITH MOST TOURISTS GONE, ROS can take every other morning off. They're sitting on a bench by the river.

"You were up early," Grayson notes.

"And you only noticed today," she responds. "I've been getting up at five all week. And, amazingly, I'm not the least tired."

"Maybe that's because you meditate."

"You know I prefer to think of it as contemplation, but yes, I agree. I didn't expect anything like this, but having my bit of quiet time gives me more energy than my longer waking hours consume. And yet, while I feel more invigorated, I'm also a lot calmer."

Grayson has noticed. He can see that she's less tense than at the café. Things don't get to her.

Ros leans back, looking at the branches reaching down, their buds no longer timidly breaking, but in the process of unfurling into vigorous leaves. "Let me ask you something, Grayson. About Hendrick."

He is mildly surprised. Is Ros interested in meditation, after all? He's also noticed that when they do talk about his past, it's now Ros that takes the initiative, and usually when he least expects it. He doesn't mind; it takes pressure off him. Grayson reaches his arm around Ros and strokes the length of her hair, first with the flat of his palm, then taking strands of it between his fingers.

"What would you like to know?" he finally responds.

"Why meeting him was such a breakthrough."

Grayson lets himself slide into the dark of his past. "I was always in control of everything. My job, the way Marlene and I built our lives. Everything. It's how I understood the world. Everything was possible, provided I took responsibility. I could control not only my destiny, but each step on its way."

"That's quite a concept."

"Not really."

"Controlling your destiny? Sounds a bit conceited to me."

"On the contrary, there's a lot of humility in it. When I say I believed I could control every step along the way, you have to realize I made them deliberately small steps."

"How do you mean?"

"You could say, my goal is to be Vice President by the end of summer. Or, two years from now I'll be in a bigger house with a swimming pool. All you'd do is set yourself up for disappointment. But you can set small realistic goals that still go way beyond what's expected from you and they'll eventually lead you toward your bigger objectives."

"Take small steps—I get it."

"It worked, for a while at least. It gave me the feeling of being in charge. The illusion, I should say."

A mother duck comes floating toward them, a flock of babies trailing behind her. They splash their way toward the bank, but when they notice Grayson and Ros they noisily dart across the water to the other side.

"I'm like those ducklings," Ros says determinedly. "Driven by instinct. Not giving my life much thought. I've always wanted to do photography full time, but doing that costs money instead of earning me a living. So I got the coffee shop to pay my bills."

"Maybe that's the better way. Your model has fewer limitations."

"How do you mean?"

"My approach worked as long as I applied the idea to external things. But then I was shot."

Ros cringes. The idea of Grayson's broken body still unsettles her.

"Afterwards, the goals I set myself were all about my body. I worked on becoming healthy again." His features harden, as he relives the disappointment. "But for months, I ended each frustrated, thinking I had no fucking chance."

"But you had to try, Grayson. What else could you do? You wanted to walk again, didn't you?"

"I fought hard for that, yes. But if everything in your life is a fight you become bitter and angry. Especially if you keep losing. Hendrick made me realize that I had to surrender at least on one level."

"How do you surrender and yet keep fighting?"

"I had to think differently. Instead of fighting my body, I worked with it. I thought of it not as something I owned, but as something that allowed me to be inside it. Which meant I had to accept it as something other than I. Accepting was the big challenge. Accepting my lot without giving up hope."

Grayson feels the energy of battle lurk near him, like a cloak of darkness, ready to envelope him again if he allows it. Going back does that. He reminds himself that he's with Ros now, in the present. But part of him is far away and when he hears his voice it's as if someone else speaks the words. "I had to hope that I would progress, but accept that I might never become fully rehabilitated," he hears himself say.

"Acceptance. That's what it's all about, Grayson, isn't it? It's the bridge."

"Hendrick would be proud of you. That was his message. Acceptance was my challenge. By accepting I'd heal myself, whether I'd be in a wheelchair or on my feet again." He pulls her close and doing so makes him feel better.

Ros suggests they walk downriver and see where the ducks have gone. It turns out they've found a quiet spot around the next bend, but as Ros and Grayson approach they scurry once more and continue their journey downriver.

Ros says, "That mother duck. I wonder if she's the one that was there when we stood on the bridge, that winter night. Remember?"

"It's when I first realized how beautiful you could be."

"I knew that was on your mind. I felt uncomfortable."

"I could tell."

Later, in bed, Ros looks down at Grayson's face as she gently rocks. His eyes are closed, but she knows the grey sadness below them. She tells Grayson of her love and he listens with his lids still shut—fragile shutters made of parchment.

She rocks some more and exhales and Grayson asks what that was about. When she says that sometimes she's afraid of what's to come, he looks up at her knowingly.

THE SPREADSHEET ON THE COMPUTER screen shows two columns, one headed SAMANTHA and the other JACK. Grayson is frustrated by his lack of progress.

When he first considered how they might divide their possessions it all seemed easy. Samantha wanted the house and he'd get most of their investments. That left the ranch land outside Carbondale and the lots in Toronto that he's leased back to the new owner of the car dealership. She'd end up with one and he with the other. But now he can see that with mortgages in place and part of it being foreign property it will be complicated. They'll need bankers and lawyers and tax advisors. Samantha won't like it. She has no patience for that kind of thing.

Worse, she'll show up any day now—probably without notice. Grayson tries to imagine what she'll look like. He knows from her note and the postcard that she's calling herself Sam again. I bet she's changed her whole image, he muses. Maybe she's had herself pierced or tattooed. He dismisses the thought: Samantha's too eager to fit into the Aspen social set. Back to short-cropped blonde, probably. That will go with 'Sam'.

Grayson focuses on the screen again. He doesn't feel good; too many things are in suspense. Last night, he's had an argument with

Ros. They talked about whether they'd move to a new place or go traveling first and Ros accused him of controlling the agenda.

"Look, whenever I start falling in love with an idea for a trip, you revert back to moving to Boulder. And when my heart gets set on Boulder, you start talking about travelling," she said. Then she accused him of being a control freak. "You always have to be in charge! The way you deal with your past, the way you plan the future. Even the way you want to coach me with my meditation."

The thing that got to him was her last comment.

"And one more thing, Grayson. The other day when you told me how Hendrick taught you about acceptance—I wonder whether you learned from it."

Grayson felt an odd sensation. He knew he could make himself understand what Ros said, but he didn't want to try.

"What I'm saying is this," Ros continued. "I've been searching my brain for some evidence of you being accepting. And I haven't found any. You don't accept things. You fight them."

Grayson loved her for her openness but hated her for taking him to this place. He stood there disoriented and unresponsive. Surprisingly, his anger stayed contained.

Later, as he was jogging through the night, he forced himself to think. He recollected Ros' words, lived through them again, placed them on an imaginary scale and weighed them.

Grayson now knows that she's right, that he tries to control things, but he can't figure out why he keeps doing it. Everything is finally going his way again. Ros is the right woman for him: he can talk to her, she's easy-going and understanding. And she cares for him, even loves him. What's his problem?

As he did last night, he searches for examples of his habit. He knows he tries to patronize her with his meditation advice.

And Ros isn't fooled by it. Besides, who is he to give her advice anyway? He hasn't followed a regular meditation routine for too long. During the past two or three years he turned inward only when something upset him. Like when Samantha annoyed him or the time when the insurance company asked him to justify his ongoing disability payments. Which was Ros' point: he used meditation when his life was at risk of spinning out of control.

He thinks back to last night. He was relieved when Ros was still awake when he came back in. She was sitting at the kitchen table, a book and a cup of hot chocolate in front of her, looking up at him and saying: "Sorry Grayson, some things have to come out."

It gave him a chance to apologize. "You're right about the control thing. I know it happens."

"It happens?"

"All right then. I do it."

"But what is it that you want to control, Grayson?"

"I have no idea. I really don't."

"Maybe it has nothing to do with us. It could be that you've had to deal with too many new things."

"Change as a threat. Let's take control of it."

"Or it could have nothing to do with the present. Maybe it's the old baggage. All that stuff with your parents. I can relate to that."

Grayson remembers saying, "No you can't. You don't know what it feels like inside me."

"Not that way. I can relate because I have similar problems with my past. My father, and Ian. I hate going there, but I know I'll get to the bottom of it. Eventually."

Grayson's immediate reaction was to take charge. "We can

explore it together, if you want," he suggested. "Talk about it." And as he said that, he understood what he was doing. Taking control. Always his first instinct.

Ros, completely unaware, deflated him again. "There's something else I need to tell you, Grayson."

"What's that?"

"No matter where we end up as a couple, I need to be independent. I'll want to have some kind of a job, apart from my photography."

Grayson keeps thinking about that last comment while he stares at the computer in front of him. The spreadsheet has disappeared. All his unfocused eyes see is the black emptiness of the dormant screen.

He's jogged at night before, but not up here. Ros is right, it's about the past, Grayson curses to himself, as he runs uphill. They had a quiet dinner, but argued again before going to sleep—or, in his case, into a state of torture scripted by his agitated mind and Ros' uncomfortably narrow bed. At eleven, Ros finally sent him to the living room to sleep on the couch, but instead he paced much of the night away. And now he's here, pushing himself up the switches of Smuggler trail.

He frequently stumbles as running shoes hit a rock or the rim of a pothole, but Grayson barely notices. There's only one message that plays in his clogged brain: I can't stop with Marlene all the time, I need to deal with my father and a dozen other unresolved things. I have to go all the way! His mind hisses endless repeats, like a steam hammer driving a mold into bits of shapeless metal in an assembly line. *Unresolved stuff. Unresolved stuff. Unresolved stuff.*

Grayson's temples throb to keep time to the hellish rhythm and his legs push one foot in front of the other, impervious to pain and maybe faster than they ever managed to on the gruelling uphill.

He has to deal with it this time. He copped out at the retreat, he can see that now. Letting things float near the surface, but then watching them drift away again, their menacing appearance changing form and turning into scattered bits of cloud dissolving into a muddy sky. It tried to come up again and again, but he purged it, thinking he'd take control. Settling into his cozy routine with Samantha instead. And with Ros it's been the same. He knows what he has to do, has never seen it more clearly than with her, yet he keeps backing off.

Ros is right: it's all about control! When he smelled gasoline he controlled that by breathing and grasping a tree or a rock. When Samantha annoyed him or his pain got him, he controlled the situation by meditating. When he couldn't follow his breath, he controlled that by chanting. Jogging, too—a control mechanism. I've got to get deeper this time, no fucking escape!

His anger feels good. He can feel the power it unleashes in him. He'll go all the way this time, go in there and fight it, like he fought for his smashed-up body. A voice from far away tries to cut in, telling him that isn't how it was: it was acceptance that worked, not fighting it. But the flush of his rage drowns the message out.

Then he hears Hendrick's voice, his words coming slowly and with great weight attached to them. 'If we don't accept it, it'll devour us.' He hears Hendrick say it one more time, his voice resonant and now he sees his teacher's chiseled face, and he thinks about the words he knows so well, and as they sink in he realizes he's never really understood. When kneeling in Hendrick's presence years ago, he saw his paralysis and his ruined family as the causes for his darkness. His focus was on reconnecting with his body and building a new life. But the monster lurking inside him now is a different one—born from the vapor of his childhood. It's not definable, but nebulous and formless and capable of striking from any direction. What if I lose, Grayson thinks, panicked, his pace slowing. What if it does devour me?

Then anger comes to his aid again, surging to new heights and lending him confidence. Let it all come to the surface, he resolves—the pain, the desperation and most importantly, the anger it all evokes. Let it come up from the deep and seek me out, so that I can see it and shatter it into a thousand fragments, and if there's more anger underneath I'll take that too. Even if anger is all there is, I'll embrace it, merge into it, let its power swell me up!

Ros is asleep when he returns. Dawn is breaking. He contemplates Ros' face in the twilight, knowing that once he plunges into his battle he'll end up hurting her like he hurt Marlene. And Ros is like Marlene. All she's trying to do is help him, while he is holding back, afraid of what lurks within him. But he's not going to lose Ros the way he lost Marlene—that's not going to happen this time. He'll protect Ros.

"No bloody way!" Ros screams. She stands against the window, the rising sun behind her, harsh and unforgiving, turning the ends of her brown hair into filaments of luminosity. "We haven't come all this way for you to go off into the desert to confront the devil!"

"Look, the reason I'm leaving is because I know what it will do to me. Trust me. You don't want to be around me." He walks up to her again, trying to hold her, but Ros pulls herself away.

"I can handle it."

"Ros, you said it yourself, so many times. I've got to confront these things I've never dealt with it. My father and all the rest." Grayson looks exhausted.

"So deal with it here. I'll be here for you. God, Grayson, it's not like I haven't been a model of patience so far."

"It's not about patience."

"You've already told me. You'll turn into some bloody missile of anger and you think I'll run away like Marlene did."

"Yes Ros. Yes!" Grayson's eyes are pleading.

"I'll tell you something. I'm not going to lose you. I'm going to be right here with you when you confront your demons. We can do this together, for God's sake."

"I've got to get out of this space. To where there are no memo-ries," he tries.

"Then we go together. All the more reason to finish our pack-ing and get out of here. In the meantime you get some sleep. You look like a bloody train-wreck. It's a miracle you didn't have a seizure up there."

"Trust me, I asked for one. A seizure. Anything."

"Go get some sleep, Grayson," Ros says, her voice softer now. "And I better go and greet the morning crowd. I'm already late." She grabs her bag and leaves. When she's halfway down the stairs she shouts, "Let it go and get some sleep, you hear?" and then the door slams.

Grayson leans back against the kitchen counter, raises his hands up to his eyes and covers them. He's too tired to think.

When Ros pulls open the curtains it's almost noon.

"Go and brush your teeth, Grayson, and then we'll sit down. I brought you a cappuccino."

Grayson rolls to the side of the bed. The sleep has helped but he could do with more. He puts on his sweatpants and walks to the kitchen table. "The coffee first, then the teeth," he says, as he sits down. "Tastes better that way."

Ros watches him take his first sip. The foam on top has collapsed into a thin white swirl that's dancing on the surface, the clumped-up cinnamon and sugar a dark smear in its centre. She says, "It's time we got away from here, Grayson. Memories everywhere, as you said this morning."

Grayson raises the cup to his lips, looking puzzled. "And where will we go?"

"You sound sad, saying that."

"Not sad, just disoriented. I've got things to finish off."

"No, you don't. You've gone to that house every day for a month. To do what? You're telling me that you're taking almost nothing, and your clothes are here anyway."

"It's not about my stuff. It's all the paperwork."

"Sit down with the professionals and tell them what you want done. It'll take one afternoon to deal with it."

Grayson stares at his coffee.

"I thought we could go into the mountains for a start. Get away from this for a while."

"We are in the mountains, Ros."

"I mean away from civilization. We get food for a couple of weeks, take packs and a tent and go off. Anna can cover me at work and look after your orchids, if you want. Apart from hiking and camping we can concentrate on our demons."

He looks at her gloomily. "My demons, Ros."

"Ours. I have demons too—you know that."

Grayson turns to the window and stares at the distance. "You don't know what you're in for," he says.

5

GRAYSON CAN'T FIGURE OUT WHY. Instead of feeling warm and self-satisfied he feels a chill. Even the Fedex man looks cold. From behind, Grayson can see his shoulders convulse. Something else is wrong: the Fedex man has got in on 34 and they're headed up. The only explanation is that he wants to deliver something to Grayson's floor.

Grayson cocks his head to see if he can read the address on the envelope. Part is obscured by the dark-blue twill sleeve of the man's uniform and the man's meticulously groomed hand, but the few letters he sees tell him what he wants to know. "I'm Mr. Grayson," he says. "That envelope you're holding is for me." But the Fedex man doesn't respond. He doesn't even turn around.

Grayson tries again. "Did you hear what…" Now the chime above the door drowns his voice out and the red light flashes 65. His floor.

The doors open silently and Grayson exits, immediately noticing that it's even colder outside the elevator. Then he remembers his envelope and turns back, but the elevator is already gone and the Fedex man is inside it. My envelope, he thinks. I have to get that envelope!

Grayson turns toward the big glass entrance doors with the

company name and logo in brushed chrome, vowing to send one of the secretaries to catch up with the Fedex man. But now the entrance is gone and where it used to be there's only a white wall. He looks around, thinking he's gone to the wrong side of the elevator lobby. But there are no doors on the opposite side either, just a small window with a light burning behind it. Grayson can't make sense of it, but he decides to walk toward it.

It takes a lot longer to get there than he's anticipated, and now he's walking in the dark, the bulb behind the window in the distance being the only source of light. He marvels at how long the elevator lobby is, deciding that it must reach all the way to the outside wall of the building. But how can the light be on the outside?

Finally, he comes close enough to see details. There are pots hanging on the other side of the window and then the dark outline of a person walks into its frame. Grayson feels grass underneath his feet now and he becomes aware that night envelopes him. He knows where he is, too: outside the kitchen window. And the person inside is his mother.

Grayson calls out to her, but she can't hear. He bends down, groping in the wet, dark grass until he finds a pebble to throw. When it hits the glass, he waves. It's me, Mom. She looks down at him and there is a flicker of recognition in her eyes. But her face stays unresponsive.

Grayson shouts, "Mom, come on Mom—you have to let me in!" Now her gaze is fixed on the sink below and her expression has become utterly apathetic.

Grayson lives through this scene a dozen times, longing to be acknowledged, trying ever new techniques to crack his mother's shell of indifference. And then he knows he's found the key, understands he can only get to her through his father. "I'm here to see Dad," he shouts and as these words leave his throat, he sees them reflected in bits of letters that dance against the night sky. They're a sickly yellowish grey and they'd resemble his handwriting if they weren't all broken.

Still, it works. There's a moment when his mother is simultaneously bent over the kitchen sink and standing at the door. Grayson turns from the window and strides toward the entrance, longing for the warmth of Mom's embrace, anticipating how he'll let his head fall against the softness of her neck. He's almost there, maybe three steps to go, when he sees her face: a glacial mask of anguish. "Dad's upstairs," he hears her say. "Why have you kept him waiting?"

Grayson sees her disappear up the steep staircase and runs after her, the chill of the night following him inside. He finds it difficult to keep up and when he arrives at the top, she's gone altogether.

Dad is sitting in his tower, watching TV, his bloated face and body colossal. He looks up at him from his recliner. From somewhere in the dark behind him, Grayson hears his mother voice once more. "Look Ed, Jack's come back to see you. After all these years."

Dad, appearing perplexed, takes a sip of root beer, then says, "Jack's in his room, sick. Been there all along."

"I know you haven't forgiven him, but he's back now. With Marlene. The two of them can take over the business now."

"Talking about Jack, go see for yourself. He's looked awful ever since he tried to run away with that woman."

"Don't go on about this old stuff now." Her voice is faint. Grayson still can't see his mother, but the way she's said that, he knows she's on the verge of tears.

His father aims his remote at the TV and mutes it. "Sick as a dog, that boy. I'm not sure he'll make it." He sounds terrible and looks worse. "He's got to eat. See if he wants a donut."

Grayson hears his mother's sob close behind him and he turns to her, his arms open. But he can't get close to her. Can't get close. Just can't.

Frost covers the grass and the clusters of gentians and columbines outside their tent. Ros wonders how anything can grow at this altitude.

"God, it's cold," she hears Grayson growl inside the tent. She bends down to see him, but he's withdrawn deep into his mummy bag. Even his hood is done up.

"Cold for summer, anyway," she answers, not sure he can hear. A few feet away, birds flutter in the bushes. Their frantic chirps fill the air. Ros listens to them for a while, realizing that there's no white noise whatsoever. The hum of construction machinery, the buzz of chainsaws, the drone of airplanes—all left behind.

She looks for a flat spot and zips up her parka, then lowers herself to her knees and closes her eyes. It doesn't take long for her to lose herself in the undisturbed cavern of her core. Occasionally thoughts drift by. They resemble different vessels on a busy river: one exotically colored, the next exuding a pungent smell, a third perfectly ordinary in shape and appearance. Sometimes Ros barely registers their presence, but at other times these thoughts create an association or evoke a memory and that causes them to intrude into her stillness. When that happens, Ros is surprised by their presence and wonders how long they've been there. She's learned to allow them to be without engaging them and found that such acceptance overwhelms them. They gently float away.

Every now and then she becomes aware of the pattern of her breath, then slips back to nothingness.

Half an hour goes by before Ros feels a sudden rush of warmth on her face. She knows the sun has risen over the ridge above them. By mid-morning the temperature will have soared from freezing to summer heat. She hears a bee hum and opens her eyes, letting herself slowly return. The spicy aroma of pine sap caresses her nostrils and the light seems impossibly bright.

When she gets back to the tent she peeks inside. Grayson is gone. She sighs deeply. Their camping trek has been good for him. He's calmer. There is little to do here, apart from hiking, preparing their simple meals on their tiny camping stove, and sitting in front of their tent or on a nearby boulder, soothed by the serenity of nature. Sometimes they just sit, and sometimes they engage in their contemplative rituals. Not because they vowed to do so, but because that's how it has evolved.

They've talked a lot too.

Ros' mind wanders to last night, each of them lying in their sleeping bag, the roof of the tent lit up by the moon just enough to let through the palest blue light. She hears Grayson tell her about his jog, about feeling his anger infuse him with strength and being tempted to surrender to it completely.

If he hadn't come back to her, he whispers to her in the cold of the mountain night, his anger would have taken him back to where he was after his accident. And denying it would have sent it back into hibernation, to reappear with even greater force in the future. He knows he must learn to accept his anger. Accept it as part of him, whether it's the manageable irritation that's accompanied him through the past years or the swelling rage he met when running up Smuggler Mountain.

Ros hears Grayson holler. He's at the creek below, splashing water on his face, part of which is still covered with shaving soap.

When he gets back they sit on a boulder and sip tea. The wisps of steam rising from their mugs catch the sunlight.

"My leg's killing me," he says. "I was dreaming again, after we talked," he said.

"Your nightmare?"

"My new nightmare. Not the Fedex man whose face I never get to see."

"I wonder who he really is, that Fedex guy."

"Let me finish. You asked me a question."

"Sorry…"

"Okay." Grayson allows his irritation to subside. "The new nightmare. The one with my father in his tower and my mother unapproachable. Ghosts, both of them."

"It's coming to the surface. You're opening yourself up."

He says nothing.

Ros considers whether she should continue. And when she allows words to form, her intonation is conciliatory, almost soothing. "Like you said, you have unresolved issues."

Again, no response.

"It's interesting you call your parents ghosts."

Grayson gets up and turns toward the tent.

"There's always this unreal quality to them," Ros continues. "Your father, as though he's condemned to act this one role of seeing the world in terms of his car dealership. And your mother like a frightened mouse. What were they like in real life?"

Grayson stares at the ground, his back to her. Ros senses

his pain, part of her wondering if she's going too far and the other already accepting blame for having done so. "I'm sorry. I shouldn't have, should I?"

His voice is choked when he responds. "It's not your fault. Or mine. It's just the idea of doing this together. I knew it would turn out like this."

"Like what?"

"It's just a fucking mistake, being here. I know what's going to happen. I'll end up taking it out on you!" And then he leaves.

Ros holds back her tears as she watches him put distance between them, first walking, then breaking into a jog. A marmot whistles, shrill and disruptive, and then there's nothing but silence, Grayson's steps now losing themselves in silence too.

Soon he's standing on a knoll, looking up at the stand of pines that rises above him. He hesitates for a moment, then runs to the tallest of the trees and puts his arms around it. Ros forces herself to watch as he sinks to his knees. She's too far away to see details but fears he may have a seizure.

Ros' notices her hands. They're close to her face and they're holding the Nikon. She has no recollection of picking it up but she understands what she is doing—she's placing the lens between herself and what can hurt. Shame joins the ache she feels for Grayson. She's decided to make herself vulnerable and instead she's creating barrier.

As her tears flow, she realizes this is a new time—something she evoked, even welcomed—and there's no way to go back to where she and Grayson were before. Her decision to come here was right, but that doesn't end her pain or lessen her fear.

GRAYSON IS GLAD HE'S CHOSEN one of the airport hotels; the trip has left him emotionally exhausted. In Denver, a 45-minute line-up followed by a security check worthy of a city under occupation, performed by grim looking, mostly overweight automatons. More waiting time at the gate, where escape from TV monitors blaring fear messages was impossible. And in Charlotte, a two-hour layover in a terminal air-conditioned to pneumonia level, with more exposure to the America's never-ending wars. At Raleigh-Durham airport, his luck finally changed. He was soaked by the time the hotel shuttle arrived at the blazing asphalt ramp, but he was the only passenger in the hotel shuttle and during the whole fifteen-minute ride the driver stayed silent.

For the hundredth time since he's sat down in the lobby, Grayson checks the time. Even wearing a watch makes him nervous. He studies its face, looks at the jerky movements of the second hand and remembers how it used to be when each of his days was governed by time.

Being here is probably a mistake. How will Martin feel about him after so many years? "He probably hates me—must have hated me every day since I left," he mumbles to himself.

Grayson tries to picture his son without resorting to the

photograph he's brought along. But he can't. Each time he tries, the face of his first-born comes up instead. Oliver's face, trying to comprehend what the nurse kneeling in front of the wheelchair is doing. Oliver looking up at his mom to find an explanation. And Oliver's eyes turning back, now filled with foreboding, still not sure what it was his father has done but knowing that he's wounded his mother.

"Would you like more coffee, sir?" The voice startles him. Any voice would. It could have been Martin's; he'll be talking in a different voice than the one he remembers. Grayson nods to the waiter and watches his cup being refilled.

He reaches for the black-and-white picture of Martin and studies it. It must have been taken on some official occasion, maybe for a high school yearbook. High school!

He's probably married now. He could be a father himself. Grayson wonders how tall his son has grown and whether he has a beard or mustache.

He asked him to send some details and an up-to-date picture. Martin wrote back and even addressed him as "Dear Dad," but his letter was only half a page long. It said that meeting at Durham would be best for him, because he was at Duke. And if it helped, he could come to the airport. They could work out the details by e-mail.

Grayson remembers waving the note at Ros, as if producing evidence that her plan was flawed. Ros shrugged it off and said he should look at the bright side. He was going to meet his son.

Why didn't Martin ask for more details, Grayson still wonders. Perhaps he could have paved the way by writing more about himself. But that thought turns sour. What could he have written? That he left his second wife? That he's still at sea? Grayson reaches into his pocket, searching for something to wipe his brow with. His hand comes out empty, then reaches for the paper napkin to the side of his coffee cup.

When the glass door opens, he knows right away that it's Martin. He's pleased that his son recognizes him too, but his joy only lasts an instant. He realizes he gave himself away by jumping up from his seat.

He feels awkward, not knowing whether he should hug Martin. But Martin solves the problem, first taking his hand and then opening his arms. His face flushes as he does so.

Grayson feels incredibly thankful as they embrace. He wants to tell his son that he looks good and healthy, but instead he says, "I didn't know whether you'd be hungry. We can stay here and have coffee or go to the restaurant."

"Coffee will be fine, thanks."

"You look great," Grayson says.

"So do you. I expected you to look older." His son smiles.

Grayson searches for words. Then his mind produces a connection. "Remember skiing together? I've done a lot of that. It keeps me young."

Martin says, "We gave it up. After you left."

"Oh. I'm sorry."

"I enjoyed skiing."

Grayson thinks he hears nostalgia in Martin's voice, then replays the three words in his mind and decides the notion was wrong. He doesn't know how to deal with this. "Maybe you can visit me some time and we can ski together again," he tries, immediately realizing that it's too early to have said that.

"Right now I'm too busy to do much traveling, Dad. Working on my Master's."

He's called him Dad! It's more than Grayson expected. He asks, "A Master's Degree in what, Martin?"

"Social Sciences. It gives me lots of flexibility, and I really haven't decided what I'm going to do."

"I see." Grayson is lost once again. He doesn't know how to move forward. "So you're at Duke…"

"Until next spring, yes."

"And then?"

"I don't know. I guess I'll move back home and start looking for a job."

"What would you like to do, Martin? As a job, I mean."

"Well, Emile—Mom's husband, you know—Emile figures that since we live in Ottawa, I may as well start with the government."

Emile. Grayson recalls his reaction when first reading the name in Marlene's letter. Asking for a divorce a mere six months after he left was enough. But marrying someone with a name like Emile? He knows his judgment is immature, but the name still nags him.

"He says if I like it, I can always go back to school and take some political science courses."

"I see. What does Emile do in Ottawa?"

"He's with the US Embassy. The military attaché."

"Ah, that's why you're studying at Duke's."

"I guess."

"How is he treating you, Martin?" Grayson asks, unsure whether he's gone too far.

But Martin doesn't seem to notice. "He's okay. He's nice to Mom, too."

"That's good to know," Grayson says emphatically and repeats it almost immediately. He's pleased, both that Marlene is well and that his sincerity is coming across. "How about your mom's health?"

"She's well, I guess."

Grayson can see that Martin hasn't thought about Marlene's medical condition lately, and he smiles. "And Oliver?"

"Oliver is fine, too. He works for the Citizen, at the foreign affairs desk."

"You must have interesting family dinners. A lot of politics for one household." Grayson feels more relaxed now.

"We don't see each other that often. Since Oliver got married, he spends more time with his in-laws. They live in Montreal."

Sadness spreads through Grayson. His chest feels like a vast hollow. "I didn't know," he manages. "When did he get married?"

"I'm sorry, Dad. It was a hard decision for Oliver. Not to invite you, I mean."

Grayson's mind is racing again, looking for words. In the end he simply says, "I know I wasn't a good father to you and Oliver."

"It was your accident, Dad."

"Still." Grayson's voice has turned scratchy. "Your mother, too. She did everything for me and I treated her horribly."

"Do you feel better now?"

"Yes, I feel good. Almost back to normal."

"Mom was telling us you got your legs back, but we didn't know much more."

"It's because I haven't been in touch. My fault." Grayson struggles. He fights to control his emotions but loses. "I feel terrible about what I did to you." Tears run down his cheeks.

Martin looks around nervously, then resolutely turns toward his father as if to purge the other people in the lobby from his mind. "You got shot, Dad. You were in a wheelchair."

Grayson puts his hand on Martin's arm. "The last time Oliver saw me, Martin…"

"He'd be happy to see you looking so well."

"No one should have a memory like that."

"After you left, it was difficult for us. We knew you were out there, alone in that wheelchair."

"More difficult for Oliver, don't you think?"

"I don't understand, Dad. Why Oliver?"

Grayson manages an excuse and runs to the bathroom, where he locks himself into a cubicle and is sick.

THE STRANDS OF HAIR THAT fall over the side of her face are speckled eggshell-white, as if bits of the paint she's using had found their way there. Ros is standing on a ladder, painting the inside of her barn. Above her are gaping, plastic-covered holes where skylights will soon be placed. The brightness that penetrates the foliage above is reflected in Ros' eyes, too: dazzling rectangles against the hazel of her irises.

She thinks of how they got here. They were on the way to check out Boulder when they realized how ideal Evergreen would be. High above the west end of Denver. Far enough from the city to escape its noise and pollution, yet close enough to take quick trips to its restaurants, movies and galleries. And just a few miles in the opposite direction, the Continental Divide, with endless hiking trails and half a dozen ski resorts.

Their property is everything they looked for. Part of the land is forested, but there are fields and meadows as well. A brook runs from the nearby ridge and empties into a pond not far from their front door. When Ros first saw it, she ran to the reeds at its edge and an army of dragonflies and damselflies emerged. Thoughts of their time in Mexico intruded, lighting up her face.

The buildings need work. Grayson has hired a small team to

upgrade the ranch house and Ros is busy with the barn. The walls are insulated and the floor is in; only the plumbing and the roof still need to be completed and she'll have the studio of her dreams!

Ros dips her roller into the tray, drains it of excess paint and lifts it to the wall. She thinks about how determined she was to get a job when they first moved here. Yet all she wants to do now is finish the renovation and get back to her photography.

Her memories of the café are bitter-sweet. She's glad to be rid of the predictability of her Aspen days, and when it comes to her former customers, she rarely wastes a thought on them. But melancholy grips her when she thinks of the sounds and smells and tastes of the café. She imagines the piercing hiss of steam and the banging of pistons filled with grinds, and her nostrils expand to welcome the heavenly smell of coffee. She contemplates the heady aroma rising from the sealed sack with the colorful foreign inscriptions that's slumped against the wall and feels her hand push deep inside and come back out with a fistful of brittle, tan beans. The coffees I have tasted, Ros muses, and the kaleidoscope of tastes of her Guatemalan favourite is on her tongue, sweet as the shade in which it's grown and powerful as the sun above the canopy of trees she imagines.

These are Anna's joys now, she reflects—sweet Anna, who always talked about returning home to Wisconsin and who jumped at the chance to buy the café.

Ros' thoughts turn to the summer it's been: difficult, and sometimes as grueling as Grayson predicted. Like the ferret she once befriended as a girl, he keeps coming out of his hole and withdraws to its safety again. Her dad had called the animal a hob, explaining to her that if it were a female she'd be a jill. She thinks of Grayson as her hob now, knowing that his progress will inch along and that her role is to keep listening. But every now and then, when he loses his way and panics, it gets difficult.

Like when he confided that he was thinking of contacting Martin. Ros hears the unhurried rhythm of his voice, hears him talk about his younger son. She sits, looking at Grayson, determined not to engage but to just be there for him, a dispassionate witness. But something she does is wrong this time—the way she nods or tilts her head. Grayson's voice turns tense, then belligerent, and Ros knows that no words, no gesture, can calm him now. She hears him accuse her of not being supportive and watches him run out of the house. He was gone for several hours.

It was hard enough for her to accept such behaviour and even more difficult not to ask questions when he returned. Even worse, she was angry with herself, questioning why she always ended up in this same position. "What the fuck have I become?" she remembers thinking. "My lover's compliant nursemaid, that's what!" It dawned on her that Grayson needed the help of a therapist, and she'd make sure to suggest that.

But she never did. Shortly after coming back, Grayson told her he recognized how fortunate he was to have her. And he said he'd get in touch with Martin.

Ros exchanges her roller for a brush and starts work on the corner where wall meets ceiling.

She expects Grayson's struggle to continue. He hasn't talked much these past days, but she knows what's happening—she hears his moans at night and feels his soaked sheets in the morning. Emotions he's suppressed for years are gradually cut loose, the chains that have kept them tied to the bottom of the dark pool of his subconscious rusting through, one by one. She understands it because it's the same for her.

Ros always thought of her father as an unimaginative, but kind man. But lately, memories she didn't know existed have crowded into her consciousness. Out of nowhere one morning came an image of her mother, her lip split and blood trickling from her mouth. Ros held the image for a long time and cried for her mother and for not being there for her.

She's also thought about Ian. Why she was attracted to an uneducated farm hand and ran away with him always puzzled her. Now she thinks she knows, mind-boggling as the apparent answer is. She fell for Ian because he reminded her of her father. And, perversely, she ran with Ian to get away from her father.

She's shared her insights with Grayson, thinking it would do her good to talk about it and hoping he would open up too. But Grayson simply listened, holding her tightly as she told him of her pregnancy, Ian's betrayal and her abortion.

Ros wonders what has brought them together and why they are here now, living under the same roof. Who is he—she asked herself that question in Aspen and in Mexico, and here in Evergreen she still doesn't know. What kind of child was he, and what would drive him if it weren't for his pain? She considers that these are the wrong questions. What am I getting out of it— perhaps that's what I need to explore. I know Grayson needs me and I know what I can give him. That's why I'm here. But it's not a strong enough reason to keep me here. What's in it for me? It's a question I really need to ask.

One thing that's clear to Ros is that she's learned to love Grayson. It's not about infatuation, this time—like with Ian and the ones who came after him. Her love didn't come without effort. That's why there's a foundation to their love, an underpinning of maturity and respect. Maybe that's all there needs to be to sustain their relationship.

And then she thinks of the test her friend Jocelyn, the psychologist, once told her about. Close your eyes and ask how you'd feel in your heart if he were in the room right now. She puts down her brush and holds on to the ladder and imagines Grayson standing at its bottom. She feels relief, even contentment, envelop her. Grayson is meeting Martin right now, but she wishes he were here.

Grayson is sitting at his desk, its curved surface filled with documents, but conspicuous order prevails. Stacks are marked by neatly printed top sheets detailing their content; individual papers are arranged by topic and priority. Running the administration of a corporation like Continental calls for meticulous organizational skills.

Grayson smells Evelyn's provocative scent near him. He suspects she's wearing it to arouse him, but he keeps his eyes on his desk.

He often looks at Evelyn. He finds her very attractive, even thinks of the two of them together, but he's never given her any indication of it and he's proud of it. Marlene is his partner and the mother of his children.

Grayson looks out over Toronto's downtown core. Apart from the heartless spike of the CN tower only four other buildings reach slightly higher than his office. He sits here because he has values. He'll never allow himself to compromise them.

"What is it, Evelyn?"

"Some correspondence I thought you'd like to see right away. And Mr. Browning would like you to come over for ten minutes."

Outside, at Evelyn's desk, the phone rings. "I'll get that," she says, and as she twirls around to leave, her smells overpower him again. He listens to her heels click on the parquet floor and hears her answer the phone. Then she stands at the door again.

"It's someone calling about your mother, Jack. Would you like to take it?"

"Yes, thank you." He waits for her to leave.

A deep voice identifies itself as his parents' physician. "I'm afraid, Mr. Grayson, your mother has had a bad fall. She's being operated on right now. She broke her hip."

Grayson doesn't ask how; he instinctively knows. Dad! He's called her up to his damned tower, probably in the middle of the night. He visualizes what happened, letting the scene play itself over, several times.

Mom holding a tray and turning toward the badly lit staircase. Then, a close-up of her foot, clad in a worn sheepskin slipper, coming down toward the step a bit too forward and at the wrong angle. There's an instant when she brings the heel down hard, trying to correct the mistake and avoid the pain which is to follow. But then a tray flies through the air and a half-full glass detaches itself and hits the wall and then Mom herself comes crashing toward him, her lower back hitting the stairs and her face convulsing. In slow motion, he watches her bounce off the oaken edges—once, twice, half a dozen times. Near the end, he observes her shoulder smashing into the wall and then he briefly thinks her neck is broken, because her head is thrown around as though only a length of twine held it to the ruined body.

Grayson remembers that he's still on the line with the doctor, but now he can't find the phone. His hands feel the walls on either side of the narrow landing, but his eyes are fixed on the top of the stairs where he thinks his mother will appear once again. Maybe next time she comes out of the tower he can warn her and all will be right. Maybe he was meant to see her fall so that he can change the course of events.

He sits down on the landing and stares, but nothing happens. And then he realizes that she can't be in the tower because she's in hospital. The doctor has told him. The moment he understands that he sees the phone again—on his desk, right in front of him. He isn't in his parents' house at all; he's in his office.

"There is one more thing, Mr. Grayson," he hears the doctor say. "Your father is alone right now. It'll be a few hours before we can get a nurse to him. Are you aware of his condition?"

Grayson wants to say something but his voice is gone. He feels his pulse quicken and notices that his hand and the pen it holds are trembling.

And then he wakes. For an instant he's relieved that it was only a dream and that Ros is lying next to him, but then he feels fury rise—the fury that always comes when he thinks of his father.

THE RENOVATION IS FINISHED. THE ripe gold of aspens covers the surrounding hillsides and the peaks behind are sprinkled with snow. It's late September. Grayson loves this time of the year. He likes to stand outside when it's still dark, long before the workers arrive, sucking in the freezing air and allowing himself to cool off to a shiver. Then he usually walks across the field that separates their ranch from the nearest ridge, marvelling at the night sky changing from black to indigo and watching even the brightest stars melt into it. By then there's enough light to see the ground and he'll break into a jog and head toward the ridge, at the top of which he'll stop and wait for the sun to touch him. Half an hour later, back home, he turns on the coffee machine and wakes Ros, as he's about to do now.

Grayson feels better than he has for a while. Looking at himself when getting up, he noticed the grey patches under his eyes, testimony to his inner upheaval. He knows he's lost weight too, perhaps too much. Yet he can tell he's making progress. He's still trying to make sense of the twisted alleys of his mind, but his searches take him deeper and he's more willing to talk to Ros.

Her suggestion to write things down was a good one. "Why

not keep notes of what you've experienced, then judge whether it's all right to share it with me," she said.

Ros is more than he could have asked for, more than he thought anyone could mean to him. It took a while, but she's learned how far she can go with him and where it's wise not to tread. And she's been true to her promise, putting up with him in his ugliest moments. Accepting him unconditionally, for what he really is.

Samantha accepted him too, but he was different then. The calm, easy-going self he projected with her was little more than a discipline of politeness and consideration. He learned to control his anger, at least temporarily, but underneath his well-mannered veneer all was chaos. Ros has helped him bring it to the surface.

He listens to her as she fusses in the bathroom, and then she enters the kitchen and smiles. Toast and coffee are waiting for her.

Ros looks at the taped-up proof of the scene she's shot outside her barn. Bits of early snow sit on the shallow ridge that marks the horizon and in the foreground, glum in its abandonment, is a lonely bale of hay, its stalks brittle in the morning cold. On the pad Ros is holding are her notes for final color corrections. She wants to get finished by the time Grayson comes over to do his weight training.

She enjoys his afternoon visits. They each do their thing, but being in each other's presence feels good.

I have to capture the light of fall, she thinks. Crisp, but not yet harsh. She goes over to the door, where she lets her feet slide into her rubber clogs. Outside, she lets nature speak for itself. She raises her eyes to the snow patches in the distance, looks back at the honey-colored bales of hay in front of her and reverts to the snow again. Now she knows that she was right. The white on her proof is too bright.

As she enters the barn again, she stands on the threshold for a moment, as if in disbelief that her working space has turned out so well. She's given up a great view to the south, but opting for skylights and north-facing windows make for ideal light. She wonders how she's ever managed to judge color in the stark light of her Aspen place.

Ros' eyes scan her new working environment and eventually settle on her desk. She walks over, takes three Tylenols from the open container and swallows them without water. She beholds the objects scattered around. Pencils and markers, notes she's written to herself, a copy of the sales contract for the café, a pair of finger-less woollen gloves. More neatly arranged where desk meets wall, are her cameras and lenses.

She still loves her Hasselblad and the two Nikons, but now she feels uneasiness when she lifts them to her eyes, finds herself checking whether she's using the camera to do more than capture an image. Ros can't recall when she first started doing it, but it doesn't matter. The important thing is that she's figured it out: she's allowed the lens to be a buffer between herself and her fears. Whatever she sees can be made better. And when she beholds imperfection, the camera separates her from it. Maybe it's the reason she got into photography in the first place.

Ros returns to her proof and tries to reconcile the beauty of her image with her reluctance to photograph new ones. She draws a blank. All she knows is that there's been a change. She spends a lot more time seeing, observing through her eyes. And she's content to work on prints that already exist.

Grayson is lying on his work-out bench, doing overheads. He exhales loudly each time his arms rise. He misses Hendrick, thinks of him almost constantly. He tries to analyze what's happening, but he questions whether he's lost the ability to be objective. Just imagining himself to be in Hendrick's presence calms the beehive of his mind.

I'm angry less often, Grayson thinks, but there are all these encounters with fear now. And perhaps delusion. *Fear—delusion, fear—delusion,* he hisses in time with his exhalations without being aware of it.

Last night's dream has led him further down his path. He was at the office, chasing from meeting to meeting, trying to get away to visit his mom in Barrie. But each time he got himself organized enough to leave, Evelyn came in and reminded him of yet another task. Phone calls came through, Browning wanted to see him and then the whole fucking board was waiting for his presentation.

That's why she died, he reminds himself. Why didn't I just leave when I got the bloody call? He realizes that his assumption of a minute ago was wrong—he still has anger in him. He can feel its lucid surge.

Grayson lowers the weights and sits up. He raises his hands to his face and digs his fingertips into his eyes, evoking the usual explosion of changing colors and shifting forms, but through it all he sees what he wanted to forget: the utter emptiness of his mother's corpse.

He feels the wet of his tears run down his fingers, as he listens to his voice say, "Why—I thought she broke her hip" and hears the nurse reply, "She was fine until this morning, but then she contracted a high fever. If only you'd come an hour earlier, Mr. Grayson."

Guilt now. Hendrick should have added it to his list. Or was guilt part of fear? Grayson reasons with himself. Maybe guilt is the fear of being held responsible for past lapses.

Thinking helps, but only briefly. Then his mother is there again. Grayson stands at the hospital bed, pulling down the sheet that's covering her. Her face is bruised: one eye socket and the jaw line below it are a purplish brown and her lips are swollen on one side. He wonders if the teeth below them are broken but doesn't have the strength to check. Images of her tumbling down the stairs flash by as he stares at her face. How much it must have hurt, he thinks, as he searches her face for an expression.

When he realizes there isn't one he's shocked. There isn't anything here that was his mom, nothing that was of her essence. That thing he's looking at isn't his mother at all. What she was has left.

Grayson remembers what he thought: that it proved there is a soul. When he feels Ros's hands settle on his back he says, "Don't, Ros."

"Don't what, Grayson?"

"Just sit with me."

She sits down next to him and sees the smears on his face. "Something to do with your dreams, right?"

"My mother," is all he says, and a long moment later, "Guilt about my mother."

They hear blasts of wind lash against the barn and see dull flakes gust past the window, Grayson sitting with the memories of his mother he has evoked and Ros considering what will happen when he gets around to his father.

The next day, as Ros returns from her barn, Grayson stands in the breezeway, holding his arms open for her. She rests her head against his chest and settles there and soon she hears his heart beat.

When Grayson says, "You know, there are days when I think I'm almost there," his voice sounds enhanced, as if he's speaking inside a vast cavern.

Something to do with the emptiness here, Ros thinks, taking in the high arched ceiling and the uncarpeted gleaming wooden floor. She takes Grayson's hand and leads him to the kitchen. "You mean with your journey?"

"Journey sounds too nice. Trip is more descriptive. A mind-trip is really what this is."

Ros nods. She asks him if they should prepare lunch together again, like they did yesterday.

"What are you thinking of?"

"It's cold in here. If you're not getting tired of stew, I'd like to try this one…" She grabs a cookbook, opens it to where she's left her mark and snuggles up to Grayson. "It requires a load of red wine, so be warned."

Grayson laughs and says he'll go down to the basement and find the right bottle. Ros wonders what he was like before his accident. As a boy, as a young married man—did he laugh a lot then? She's been thinking about the real Grayson lately: what would there be if you stripped away the identity that circumstance sprung on him, that he embraced so eagerly? What would reveal itself? Intuitively, she knows she likes the real Grayson. Loves him.

When he returns with two bottles he says cheerfully, "One to cook with, one to drink. If the workers were still here, they'd be talking."

Unlike most of Ros' and Grayson's culinary creations, the stew turns out superbly. They joke about it, deciding that theirs is the only example of two cooks producing a decent meal.

As they stand at the kitchen counter, occasionally opening the lid to stir or add more wine, Ros returns to their conversation.

"Grayson, I've been thinking about who we really are."

"I think about it all the time—about who I am, at least. Or who I may be."

"Those workmen, when I listened to you laugh or talk to them, I felt very close to who you really are. It felt good."

"We have to interact, plus I'm learning. I'm starting to get an idea of what tools I'll need at my workstation in the barn. I'm never going to be a carpenter, but maybe I'll be able to fix things."

"It's more than that, Grayson—there's more to your interactions."

"Part of my true identity, you think. Me, the recluse?" There's an edge to his words.

"Yes, as opposed to the identity we acquire. Corporate executive or artist, that kind of thing."

"Or shooting victim who can't relate to the world around him?"

Ros cautiously says, "That too."

There's a long moment of silence before Grayson continues. "When that seer took me back in time, I realized that I'd settled into a routine which sheltered me from reality. I lived in a house that could accommodate a small army, Samantha and I took shelter in small-talk, and so on. It could have lasted the rest of my life."

"And what's reality?"

"I guess it's the same for everyone. Who am I? And where am I going?

Ros opens the pot and stirs, then says, "Troubling questions, those. And how about, what can I do to make my life meaningful? To feel proud and useful?"

Grayson laughs. "That comes later. I'm still working on the first one."

"Who am I?"

"Yes. It's taking me a long time."

"That's true of anybody, don't you think? And besides, who asks that question? Most people don't even want to go there. You know, you're making progress, Grayson. The thing with your mom the other day, I could feel your pain then. But ever since, I've sensed the relief it brought you."

"I don't know. Like I said, there are times when I think I'm almost there."

Ros suggests they should have a toast and starts pouring the wine, when the phone rings. She watches Grayson look for the handset, nearly knocking over one of the orchids he's brought along. Eventually he picks it up from one of the bookshelves. She hears him say that, yes, this is Mr. Grayson, and then a faint stream of high-pitched chatter reaches her ear. She watches him write down things and finally he says he'll call in next week and hangs up.

"What was that?" Ros asks.

"The insurance company. They want to schedule their annual attempt to discontinue my ongoing disability."

"Can't you just get the doctor to verify that you're eligible?"

"No, they insist it has to be one of their chosen doctors. It's the same guy in Denver I saw before."

Ros walks to him, their two glasses in hand. "We haven't had our cooks' tot yet." She snuggles up against him. "Let's get nicely soused and spend the rest of the day in bed."

"Snoring, at this rate," says Grayson, and they clink their glasses.

They go and sit at the table and look out at the low clouds racing eastward. Occasionally, a gust sends a swirl of snow from the roof above them and they watch it blend into the background.

"Who are you really, Grayson?"

"Who do you think?"

"I remember at the café once, a long time ago. Thinking about how you were different."

"And?"

"You talked differently than others. Less rushed. The town employees and trades people would get up and say, I gotta be out of here. Fred Benning would say, I need to be in court. Pompous asses—what they meant is, get over to my table right now and get paid."

"What did I say?"

"Before we knew each other better, the same thing every time. You'd wait until I looked your way and simply asked if you could pay. And when I came over you looked a bit awkward, as if you felt bad for disrupting my routine."

"And what does that tell you?"

"That you're different. More sensitive than the others."

"Not much of a clue to my real self."

Ros considers. "Still, I was reading you correctly. You are sensitive."

"What about that other thing. The one you called the identity we build for ourselves?"

"I think it starts with our family, with teachers and societal rules. We're told what we should be in order to be considered successful."

"So it's their expectations that determine who we want to be. How we want to present ourselves."

"A bit more, actually."

"How do you mean?"

"I think it goes like this, Grayson. We feel our parents or teachers have expectations. But those expectations aren't always what we believe them to be. So, it's not what the world wants from us, but what we believe it expects that determines what identity we take on."

"What about later? After we grow up?"

"I suppose circumstances determine how we change."

"Like my accident?"

"Yes. That's an extreme example, so it caused extreme adjustments."

"Wheelchair man, although that's past. Let's use ex-father."

Ros pauses to think. "The important thing is to know that those things aren't your real self," she says eventually.

"They seem real enough to me."

Ros places her hands on his. "They appear so real because you're attached to them. You like your self-image as a father."

"Don't go there, Ros."

"All right, maybe it's not fair in your case."

"My case? What's it got to do with my case? Every man who has kids wants to be a good father."

"Yes, but in your case the father identity you picked for yourself was wrested away from you. By circumstance."

"Oh, Christ, Ros. This is bullshit. I didn't pick that identity, it just came with having kids. And no, that identity, as you call it, wasn't taken away by some circumstance. I fucking blew it with my family, all by myself."

Ros knows to pull back. She lets her fingers search the surface of his hand and feels him resist for a moment. And then his muscles loosen and she hopes she can convey her meaning. I'm here for you, her fingers say, probing his veins and the wrinkled valleys between and stroking his knuckles. I'm here and always will be.

"When you were a dad," she continues softly, "what do you think you did best with your sons?"

Grayson loves Ros' voice when it's like this. Melodic and bubbly like the ice-covered river below the bridge they stood on in Aspen. Calm like the murmur of water. He cherishes the sensation, lets moments go by. Then he thinks about her question. "Christ, I've never thought about that. I guess I was a good provider. Worked hard to make things good for them."

"Providing, working hard," Ros says softly. "Those are the things you were taught a responsible father had to do." She keeps her hands on his as if to stay in touch with the pulse of his emotions. A fox dashes across the field outside, its body impossibly slender and its tail held high.

Grayson's expression turns dull, like the wintry sky outside. "You mean, did I spend a lot of time with them?"

"No. I just want you to think of what you did best."

"Christ, Ros. Life was a flurry then. I worked so damned hard." He reaches for the bottle, adds wine to their glasses. "I suppose skiing meant a lot to them. We did that together. The winter before I got shot."

GRAYSON HOLDS THE ENVELOPE FROM Samantha as though he could assess its contents by weighing it. It's addressed to him at the Aspen house, but has been forwarded to Evergreen along with his other mail. Obviously the letter he sent to India a few weeks ago didn't make it, or Samantha would know he's moved.

He tears the envelope open, holding on to it for a moment to glance at the ridiculously large exotic stamps, before putting it down. And now both his hands are clasping the letter, unmistakably in Samantha's handwriting, the characters graceful and rounded. He wonders what life for Samantha is like.

Dear Jack.

A lot of time has passed since I last wrote, but time is of no meaning here. We once experienced something like this together, so you'll be able to relate. Hours meet hours and days become weeks, seamlessly like at Hendrick's retreat. The only difference is that all is lush and moist here—an ideal climate for abundant birth and speedy decay.

The Colorado contingent is long gone and most of the people at the ashram are now German and Dutch. They seem to approach spiritual practice with a zeal that would surprise our American friends. Even when we're not in silence, they stare in front of themselves and insist on not communicating.

One wonderful exception is Veronika, a girl from Denmark. She and I have become good friends and despite our considerable difference in age we have a lot in common—it feels as if we had been very close in a previous life!

We walk, spend a lot of quiet time together, and sometimes read to each other. Last week, we decided to share a room and made a commitment to each other that we'd stay at least three months longer. Perhaps we'll even go travelling together. India is so vast and I have seen nothing so far, being confined to the ashram. All I get to see occasionally is Maddur, a town nearby where our truck goes to pick up staples once a week. A few times I went along.

The heat here is unimaginable. The rooms at the ashrams are relatively comfortable—they're mud construction, but it does a good job of keeping out the heat. Spending twenty minutes in the open is nearly impossible, though.

Luckily, we're told the worst is behind us. In a few weeks it'll turn cooler and from that perspective our idea of travelling may be timely.

His Holiness is as inspiring as ever and being in his presence always touches my soul at the deepest level. It is hard here to imagine the world not being perfection. This is heaven on earth—it really is! I will definitely come back here once a year, as many people from all over the world do.

Jack, I have thought much about the life we led and there are things I can now see more clearly. One is that I was forever mistaking sensuous experiences with spirituality. My beauty treatments and spa visits now seem preposterous. I have made up my mind that when I'm back I will give the money I would have spent in Aspen and have no way of spending here to the ashram. And I think I'll live a simpler life—we'll see if I can manage that.

Also, I've given more thought to the house. Frankly, I am no longer sure I want it. But keep on treating it as if it were mine, because I know I am quite capable of changing my mind again when I return. Having said that, I don't even know if you're still in Aspen, but it's the only address I have.

And finally, Jack, you are forgiven. You and I were just not on the same page in the great book of life, as my friend Veronika says it. It's better we parted now than later, because our time here is limited and we still have a lot of growing to do, both of us. I feel close to you still and I think of you as I would of the darling brother I've never had.

Love,

Sam.

PS: You've probably noticed the transfers from our joint account. I told them to send me $1,500 each month. Life is inexpensive here.
PPS: Jack, because of what I wrote earlier you've probably met with lawyers to prepare a separation agreement. You've always treated me fairly, so I trust you totally. But can we leave the signing of all this until I return?

Relief overwhelms Grayson—relief that Samantha is so accepting and that things are going well for her. And there is another emotion, something between amazement and awe. He's underestimated Samantha's capacity to question her lifestyle and embark on a quest for truth.

His thoughts turn to the retreat. He sees himself in the dining hall the first time, friendless and miserable, the identity he thought was the real Grayson obliterated and nothing there yet to take its place. Someone who once was.

Samantha was there and helped me, he says to himself, and feels unworthy. He failed her, left her so he could be with Ros. And he'll probably end up failing Ros too, even though things are going well right now.

What would Hendrick say, how would he judge me? It takes but an instant for Grayson to know that Hendrick wouldn't judge—he would accept. He accepted all and everyone, Hendrick did. Giving marks for correct living or tips on how to go forward was not part of his approach.

But neither these thoughts nor the tears he sheds make Grayson feel better.

His talk with Ros has helped. She may not see it that way, but Grayson now knows he wasn't much of a father. What he used to say to his colleagues at work sums it all up: Marlene's in charge of house and children, and I'm responsible for making it all possible. The one good thing is he understands what has to happen next.

He puts down the bag with brackets that will hold the shelves he's installing in the garage. It's a job he can do himself and likes. The mindless tasks he's been setting himself help. They give his mind time to wander, his thoughts time to percolate.

And Ros, what would he do without her? She's capable of broaching topics he's never thought of, but always finds a way to guide him back to the issue that matters. So subtly he doesn't notice until it stares him in the face.

Grayson's thoughts turn to their talk about life's milestones and how they didn't much matter. It was the in betweens that counted. He tries to apply the principle to his fatherhood. What if Oliver and Martin wrote his obituary? He was a great provider, he knows that. His constant promotions secured the house, nice holidays and private school. But what did that mean to them? Who was he to his sons? Did he crawl around on the floor sharing their toys with them, or even make them toys? Was he there when they had problems with their homework? Grayson cringes. He must have been as indistinct and remote a presence to Oliver and Martin as his father was to him.

That's why he needs to get close to Martin—he understands the need for that. Getting back into Martin's life and being there for him will be his mission. Christ, he's been asking himself what could make his life more meaningful, make him feel proud. And here it is, has been for years, right in front of his eyes. Martin will be the start. And maybe through Martin, he can become part of Oliver's life as well.

Grayson knows the time is right to go upstairs and start what he's vowed to do: write another letter. He puts drill and hammer into his tool bucket and leaves the garage.

He's scribbling on a pad, considering different beginnings. What is it he really wants to say? Again and again, he looks at the reply he's received from Martin and contemplates its messages.

Grayson reflects on how difficult he found it to sum up his feelings after he met his son at Durham. Each time he sat down to write, the scene of Marlene and Oliver walking in on him and Celia played out. He felt disgusted with himself. Even if Oliver didn't understand, he must have sensed that something terrible happened.

At their meeting, Martin had given him a glimpse into how he felt. "You got shot, dad. You were in a wheelchair." And some of the passages in the letter sound the same. They'd come to understand, or at least accept, his pain.

Eventually Grayson decided to be as blunt as he could. Without reciting the distasteful details, he told Martin that he understood how heartlessly he'd treated them all and how, driven by his black anger, he had managed to lose them—lose his family. Later in the letter, after explaining his anguish and begging for forgiveness, he asked Martin whether he thought Oliver would like to see him.

He can't blame Martin for being equally direct. His words trouble Grayson, but he knows he was the one who set the stage. Once more, he reads.

Dear Dad,

I too feel good about meeting you after all this time, and I want to thank you for coming all the way here to Durham. I know it was a long way for you!

I am now in the midst of a lot of schoolwork but I wanted to respond to some things you brought up right away. I sense a lot of anxiety in your words and so it's better if we clear the air.

Dad, the time after your accident was a difficult one for all of us, but nowhere near as grueling as it must have been for you. We missed you, but after a time, life went on for Mom and Oliver and me. We coped in our own way. Mom found Emile and I think she's happy with him. Oliver and I went off to boarding school and then university and each of us learned to be independent. We both excelled at things like debating, and Oliver is a great athlete as well.

When we met I got the feeling that you had found a good new life too. Living in Colorado must be great and you said you skied a lot, which I know you like. You didn't talk about your wife, but Mom always told us that she must be the right for you, so I hope your life is a good as ours.

Finally, you asked me if I thought Oliver would like to meet with you too. I want to give you an honest answer and I hope that is what you'd like me to do. Maybe starting a correspondence with him would be a better idea for now.

I will be very busy the next while, but please feel free to write again.

Yours,
Martin

Grayson's eyes return to the passage that stirs him most. *The time was a difficult one for us,* and *I hope your life is as good as ours.* Is Martin trying to build a barrier? Grayson can't tell, but it's apparent that his son sees himself as part of a family that no longer includes him, Jack Grayson. Should that come as a surprise? Grayson concludes that it was inevitable.

And what about the last point, that it would be better for him to write to Oliver? Is Martin just speculating that a meeting would be premature or does he actually know? Maybe they've already talked about it; maybe Emile was part of the damned discussion. Emile, the military attaché—the guy's got to be a pretentious prick, Grayson just knows it.

He catches himself, realizing that's a cruel judgment of the man who's been there for Marlene and his sons. He decides he needs to be positive to get anywhere with this, disappointments notwithstanding. He goes on reading fragments of Martin's letter, weighing sentences and pondering words, until his emotions become blunted, like scalpels that have been used on too many hearts.

He's no nearer to responding than he was yesterday or the day before and so he decides to wait before putting on paper what must be said. That he's no longer with Samantha but now lives with Ros, and that he now knows he wasn't there for Martin and Oliver even before his accident.

ROS IS LAYING ON THE wooden floor of the barn. It's where she has her quiet time when it's rainy outside. Although her eyes are now closed, she's found stillness while watching the swirl of clouds through the skylights.

The bustle that is her morning routine is long forgotten and she's even managed to escape her headache. Occasionally a thought floats by. She's learned there is nothing wrong with that, as long as she doesn't connect with it. She tries to treat thoughts like sailboats on an ocean she's watching. They're always there, distant white specks on the horizon, yet they don't distract from the magnificent vastness of the sea. There is no need to ask who might be on the sailboats, who built them, whether the sailors are busy scrubbing the deck or have taken an afternoon off.

When she allows herself to come out of it, Ros slowly rolls onto her stomach and gets on her knees. Then she starts with the last part of her morning practice, her affirmations. They've become like old friends. She doesn't have to concentrate on them or remind herself of their essence. They're simply there, slowly drifting past her, their sequence a ritual that doesn't require thinking.

Let me be humble, she starts, and imagines the splendour of a meadow in spring. All is promise here, budding and blossoming and assuming color. Some leaves hold drops of dew that reflect the changing sunlight, others are so thin that the light shines through them. Visualizing nature makes Ros content, but also aware of her insignificance. Perhaps the two emotions are related.

Let me listen, comes next, and she visits the place in the forest she knows. There are things to see everywhere: the sunlit dust on the path, the greens of moss and dazzling rusts of lichens. And the things she sees make thoughts come rushing in, some bringing connections and others evoking memories—thoughts of great contentment and thoughts of regret. Let me listen better, she says to herself and hears the rushing creek in the background and the chirping of a squirrel and much nearer the chattering of birds and the wingbeat of a fly. And let me listen to people, too, she thinks after a while, knowing what a challenge that is. Not that she's an incorrigible talker—she just finds it hard to listen and she knows she misses a great many insights others have to give.

That leads to her next affirmation, which is to accept and not judge, and Ros reflects on how difficult that is for her. Her face radiates as she goes through the routine. She knows her weaknesses so well, they've become friends. That's what her practice has done for her: she's learned to accept herself. Let me be accepting and not judge, she repeats, and without her being distracted by them, scenes from the café in Aspen float by. People are coming to buy their latte or cappuccino and she's behind the counter, judging them the instance she sees them. She smiles, thinking it funny that she does that and she's thankful that she knows it.

Let me reach out to people. Ah, that's the most difficult thing for her. The image of Grayson transpires and she thanks him for showing her the way. Grayson reaches out; he's reached out to her and that's how they met and got together. And now she watches him talk to the carpenters working on the barn, asking them if they have children, where they live. What blessings touching others could bring!

Somewhere far in the distance is the thought of how Grayson, too, had to learn opening himself to others, was forced to learn it after his horrible accident. She imagines the Fedex man and others from Grayson's earlier life and a fleeting sadness overcomes her because she knows how many times Grayson has cried over his lack of interest and compassion.

And then Ros moves on to the part where she wants to be part of all that is. All humans, all grasses and trees and blossoms, the rivers which course through the world and the wet black loam of her vegetable beds, the worms that live in it and the robins that pull the worms from the ground when it rains. She feels the energy of the gurgling brook that leads to the pond and feeds the reeds and grasses by its bank that are home to the dragonflies she loves. And she thinks of the pebbles which hurt the soles of her feet when they get caught in her clogs and the stones she picks from between the flowers and the sand of the red deserts she's seen in Utah, New Mexico and Arizona. Let me be part of it all, she wishes. No, let me be one with all!

And this is always when she feels best, no longer alone or alone with Grayson, but integrated into one creation that lives itself through her, a world that's singing with the awareness of its perfection and that is singing with one voice.

Only one part remains to Ros' affirmations, the part where she resolves to be aware and mindful. Of all things, becoming more mindful had been the most difficult for her, even though she once thought there was nothing to it. Each time she finishes her ritual, a flurry of thoughts and concerns overcome her and the stillness is gone. Even when she works on her photography, her mind is no more at rest than when she cooks or works in the house or talks to Grayson.

The only time she's truly mindful is when they make love, and as the image of her and Grayson together fills her mind, she wants him with her, wants him to initiate the moves that made up their heavenly ritual, so that she can let go and take it all in. Yes, let me be mindful, the way I am when I'm with Grayson. She dwells on this thought for a minute, her breath quickening with the excitement of it, and then lets it gently float away.

And then she comes to the end: let me be thankful. But more than just one thought or resolution, this last one is a composite of all the others, for if she listens and opens herself up, and if she's humble and doesn't judge, and most of all, if she's one with all and mindful, then her soul will soar and gratefulness for what she has will be present.

Her brain makes her see a mist of pink and light green swirling from her chest, as she dwells on what is good in her life—the colors of the heart. Pink for the life force suffused with love, light green the hue of all things that grow. She feels a wave of immense contentment and she slightly bows. Thank you for the barn and the ranch and the pond and the fields next to it, and thank you for photography. And most of, thank you for Grayson—my wonderful Grayson who's struggling, and despite that manages to show me kindness.

Ros gets up, feeling a bit wobbly. She focuses on the stiffness in her knees first, but then she becomes aware of her headache again.

She hasn't slept well. It's still night when she makes herself a mug of mint tea and takes it outside. On the porch, Ros settles in the wicker chair cloaks herself with her chequered blanket.

Before long, her eyes settle on the round shroud of grey hanging low in the dawn sky. Inside rests a white sliver of moon, veiled in moisture like a fetus in its amniotic membrane. To Ros this embryonic moon holds a promise as vast as the dark space into which it will grow. And she can tell that the moon knows of its own potential too, is aware that the earth's shadow will shrink and eventually lift and thus allow it dominance of the sky.

Later, Grayson will join her on the porch, but by then the possibilities of the dawn sky will have vanished into the blandness of a drab light that is neither night nor day.

GRAYSON HAS AN HOUR TO kill. He thinks there is a Starbucks a few doors down, but he's wrong. Instead, he ends up in a pub, where he settles into a booth by the window and orders a beer he's never heard of.

He's no longer used to the activity he sees outside. Aspen was a small town, but there was always someone walking around. On the ranch outside Evergreen he gets to see few people other than the construction workers busy with their renovation. Boulder is a hive of activity by comparison; the sidewalk Grayson looks out on and the street behind it are those of a thriving city.

He takes off his jacket and slings it over the back of the chair next to him. Then he remembers his wallet and Martin's picture inside. He wonders why he feels like looking at it—the image he carries in his head is much truer to the Martin he's about to meet than the wallet-sized high school photograph. Grayson realizes he's nervous, even more so than he was before their meeting in Durham. The stakes are larger too.

A disheveled looking man grins at him from across a nearby table—the only other guest at this hour. Grayson labels him: somewhere between sixty-five and eighty, unshaven, suit and tie rumpled and on closer inspection most likely stained. A retired clerk living alone. All this goes on in the space of a second at most and Grayson isn't even conscious of it.

"Killing time?" the old man asks. Grayson expected his voice to be throaty. Instead it's shrill.

"I guess," Grayson replies, trying not to engage in some meaningless pub discourse. He wants to be ready to meet his son.

"I could tell right away. You know why?"

"It's obvious," Grayson shoots back. "What else would I be doing here in the early afternoon?" He realizes he's fallen into the trap. Each reply will draw him in deeper.

The old man surprises him. "I can see you want to be alone. Just to get this thing straight, though. My father spent every afternoon in this place and not to kill time. It's where he conducted his business. Never saw him at home."

Grayson errs again, muttering he's sorry.

"Sorry? You don't have to be sorry for me."

"I didn't mean it that way."

The old man ignores him. "What he did here put me through college and beyond. PhD in engineering. Not that you'll believe me, the way I look." He takes his cap off, revealing a few wisps of grey hair.

Grayson is intrigued, but not sufficiently to want to stay. He takes an immense gulp, emptying a third of his pint-sized glass and nervously looking around for the waitress. "Interesting story," he says. "But I've got to get going."

"If you were younger, I'd say you're off to meet a woman," the old man says. "You're nervous enough. But at your age, more likely to see a son or daughter."

Grayson shakes his head, amused. "That's pretty good. I'm off to meet my son."

The man mumbles something to himself, gets up, and with beer in hand comes over to Grayson's booth. "In case we meet again, Richard McAuley," he says, holding out his hand. "People call me Rich."

"Then you're a regular."

Rich points at his mug. "This is my first one today. By the sixth or seventh, around dinner time, I'll have seen all my buddies. But you, you're not from around here."

"No." Grayson wonders what he's getting into. "No, I'm not."

"And your son? He's at college here?"

"No, he's here for the day on an assignment. Part of his Master's at Duke's. Apparently, Boulder has some unusual characteristics as American cities go."

"Tell me about it. Between the panhandlers and the socialist millionaires who keep them in style, we've got everything. There's only one prerequisite to living in Boulder. You need to be politically correct. If you're not, you end up living right here, in this pub."

Grayson grins.

"My father spent his day and night here, gambling. It wasn't a pub then. A private house, open to whoever knew what went on inside. His stick was telling stories. He used them on pretty women or to rope the men into a game. Most didn't mind losing a week's pay because his stories were so damned good. Not a single word true, I suspect."

"He must have been a character," Grayson says without conviction.

"I didn't see him that often, but when he made an appearance everything changed. He lifted me up and sat me on his knees and as he spun his tale, I thought I was right there, rafting down the Zambezi on a raft with him. Or wrestling with a Boa in the Amazon."

Grayson wants to leave, but curiosity keeps him.

"Yes. Meanwhile, my mother could have taken me to the darkest Africa and I would have never known it. It would have been no different than visiting Aunt Selma in Colorado Springs." The old man rolls his eyes.

"So you adored your dad."

"I wanted to run away with him more than anything. Or sit on his knees and listen to stories, forever."

"But you went to school instead."

"By then I knew he was a gambler and womanizer." Rich lifts his glass and drinks, then smacks his lips. "Once, when feeling sorry for my mother, I told her what I thought of him. But she wouldn't have any of it. Told me there was enough cash in the bank box to put me through college and buy me a big house when I graduated. And only she had a key."

"I guess he understood his weakness."

"We all do, I think, at some level. Mine is beer and hanging out in this hole." Bits of spittle settle on the polished table as he laughs.

Grayson gets up. "Listen, Rich, I need to move on—be there when my son gets in." He looks at the tab the waitress left next to his glass and counts out some bills. "I enjoyed meeting you." He sounds awkward.

Rich tilts his head sideways and says, "Next time we meet you tell me your story. Damn, I didn't even get your name."

"Grayson. Jack Grayson."

"Well, look after that son of yours, Jack. Be good to him. No matter how old, a fellow always needs his father."

The Highlander is moving slowly, but its tires are spitting bits of gravel and kicking up dust. Ros is standing on the porch watching Grayson drive up.

As he walks up to her she can tell he's troubled, even though he forces a smile. She reminds herself to go easy. "How was traffic?"

"Congested. But what's 35 miles?" Grayson says, as he walks by her and disappears into the house.

Dinner is an experiment, a pheasant one of their new neighbors brought over as a welcoming gift. Ros put it out to thaw last night, placed it in marinade in the morning and stuffed it when Grayson was gone. She enjoys cooking now; the creativity of planning and making a meal satisfies her. And she's surprised by how fast she's learning. "How about picking a good wine," she instructs Grayson.

When he returns Grayson is holding two bottles of Pinot Noir. He says, "I can tell you know it wasn't a success. You would have asked otherwise."

"I'm getting better at reading you, Grayson."

"You are getting good at dealing with me. I'm a lucky man."

She turns, nestles against him and whispers, "I'm sorry."

He answers, "I'll get over it" and leaves it at that. He gets a knife and holds its blade against the aluminium foil, then with the other hand starts turning the bottle. A round bit of red tin careens onto the counter and rolls a few inches. Ros is relieved that he's busy with the wine, saying she can't wait to get a taste of it.

"Then hand me the corkscrew, will you?"

Ros' hand reaches into the drawer and comes out holding a black screw-pull.

"The problem is I'm kind of stuck. I know I want to have a relationship with him, but he doesn't seem interested. At least I didn't fly to Durham this time."

"What makes you think Martin's not interested?"

"I could tell. The whole thing lasted forty minutes and I learned more about his assignment than about him."

"I see."

"You know, Ros, I got there way too early and ended up waiting in a pub. There was an old guy—he and I the only customers in the whole big place—and he came over to chat. I know more about him than I do about my son."

The carmine liquid gushes into their glasses with joyful prattle, but Ros hears only the echo of Grayson's words. She can tell he's wounded. "What is it you'd like to know about Martin?" she tries.

Grayson considers. "It's not so much about knowing details. More that we didn't have a real talk."

"All right then. What would you have wanted him to talk about, Grayson?"

"What kind of a relationship he's in. What his passions and problems are—that kind of thing. Or how his mom and brother feel about me. That jibe in his letter didn't help, I guess."

"What jibe?" Ros lifts her glass and sips without noticing.

"Where I asked if he thought Oliver would be interested in seeing me and he answered no, it would probably be better if I tried writing."

"Did you ask him about it?"

"Not directly, no." He throws up his hands dismissively. "I'm not sure this damn thing is even worth discussing."

Ros bends down, opens the oven door and peeks inside. "A while to go yet," she says to herself. She weighs her next words while she watches Grayson refill his glass. "What I get from this is that you're disappointed because of what Martin didn't say. Or is there something he said that hurt you?"

Grayson takes another gulp. He looks at Ros as if there was something in her question that greatly bewildered him. "That's a good question. You always amaze me."

"Why?"

"Your intuitive capacity."

"Tell me."

"There was something he said that rankles. Now that I think about it, yes—that was probably the thing that disappointed me most."

"And what did he say, Grayson?"

"It was when we were leaving. I told him I'd like to learn more about him and suggested another meeting. I could come to Durham or anywhere else." Grayson reaches down to pick up the corkscrew again, starts playing with it, forcing it deeper into the wine-soaked cork that's attached to it.

"That was generous."

He looks up at Ros.

"Well, how did he respond?"

"He said he probably couldn't for the next several months. That he was too busy with his master's thesis."

"Those were his words?"

"That's what he said." Grayson walks over to the window and looks out at the dense ashen clouds that blanket the ridge at the far end of the field. "For a few seconds I couldn't think. I felt numb. Christ, I was fighting back tears. Here I finally moved my life into a positive direction and I was failing. We hugged stiffly and he started walking away, and then the paralysis wore off and I thought, no, I can't allow that."

Ros watches him from behind as she has so many times, his outline almost blending into the dull light of the concealed sky.

"I went after him and said, look, I can't accept what you said, Martin. I'm suggesting we take three or four hours out of the next couple of months and you tell me you don't have time for that?"

"And?"

"And that's when it came out."

Ros waits for him to continue, but he's silent, just standing at that big window staring out.

"What came out, Grayson?" she asks softly.

"At first he stuck to his story—his workload, all that shit. But then he said it how it is. He was feeling overwhelmed by me suddenly being in his life and had to think about it. I said, what's there to think about? We're father and son, it's that simple."

"And then?"

"He kind of lost it. In a polite way. No screaming, but a lot of pent-up emotion. I could tell. He said if it was that simple, then where the hell had I been all these years?"

It's interesting what Sundays do to people. Grayson and Ros have the freedom to live their week any way they want to, but it's invariably on a Sunday when they take extra time for each other. Their usual routine is to go exploring their new surroundings, Grayson wearing his backpack, stuffed with sandwiches, fruit, a large thermos of tea, rain gear and a warm blanket.

This Sunday is spectacular. The sky is cloudless and the light of a transcendence that only exists at high altitude. Hills and peaks fifty miles away appear in the sharpest focus and take on new meaning. Ros has tried to capture this sensation on film many times, but the results are invariably disappointing. The effect seems too contrived and she ends up dulling the colors.

By mid-morning the backpack and Grayson are ready to go, but Ros isn't. Her headache is back, more persistent and raw than ever. Grayson can see her agony; there are times when she seems close to passing out.

He reassures her, tells her he'll make her better, then moves one of the oversized leather chairs to the fireplace and helps her settle into it. He goes upstairs and returns with a quilt which he spreads across her. When he asks if she'd like hot chocolate, she manages a strained smile.

Later he joins and cuddles her. They lie near the fire, hypnotized by its ecstatic display until its sputtering flicker dies down, and then they're mesmerized anew—this time by the bed of pulsating embers, their radiant throbs signals of faith that somehow, against all odds, they will be saved from turning to cold ash. And yet, while they lay dying their heat is more noticeable than ever, a reminder of the passion of life and the strength of hope.

Grayson feels Ros' leg twitch against his and as he looks to see if she's asleep, he notices his hand. It keeps stroking Ros' lustrous hair. He turns his head to kiss the strand of auburn between his fingers. And then he gets up as gently as he can.

As he walks down the hall toward his office, his mind is already on Martin. He's not going to walk away from this. He'll find a way to get closer to his son. His sons, he corrects himself. First Martin, then Oliver.

6

IT'S THEIR FOURTH TRIP TO Denver. Grayson hopes Ros will get a definitive diagnosis. There is nothing worse than being sent from one specialist to another. With a bit of luck, they can get whatever X-rays or scans she needs on this visit. If not, they'll drive home and return once more.

The trip to the city isn't long, but Grayson hates the crowded highway, especially where it skirts miles of grimy industrial buildings. He could have stayed off I-70, but then he would have encountered dozens of traffic lights. Come to think of it, he dislikes leaving the ranch. He and Ros have settled into a comfortable routine.

"How are you feeling?" he asks Ros, squinting into the low morning sun.

"Great today. That's what's so perplexing. I'm close to collapsing for a few hours, then I'm all right again."

"You did collapse, Ros."

"Yes. Don't I know it."

Grayson turns South onto I-25. Only a couple of miles now. He thinks of her body slumped on the studio floor, a blown-up proof crumpled under her and shards of a mug in a puddle of tea near her feet. For a moment he thought she was dead. A heart attack or an aneurysm.

Now he feels a bit better. Getting an appointment with this Kepperling fellow at such short notice was lucky. Grayson checks the time. It's ten to nine; they'll be there on time.

The meeting with the doctor is inconclusive. Kepperling is much like Grayson imagined him. Middle-aged. Polite but distant. He even wears a white coat. He asks Ros how long the pain has been there, how it first manifested itself, where it hurts. And when Ros has answered these questions, there's follow-up. Has she experienced any changes in her sensory perceptions, how often has she fallen, and did she lose consciousness when she fell?

Then a rudimentary examination. Move your pupils. Open, close and wiggle your jaw. Turn your head in various directions. Does this hurt and can you feel that? It lasts 50 minutes and then Ros is told to see the receptionist. She'll be told about where to go for the tests, that's how he says it. You'll be told, Ms. Dexter. A dyed-in-the-wool bureaucrat, after all. Grayson is starting to dislike Kepperling, world-class specialist that he may be.

Outside, at the desk, the receptionist gives Grayson a map with directions. She's talking too fast for him to follow, but the clinic is circled and he's sure he'll find it. He is told there is no point in him waiting while Ros is being tested. Then more instructions. Who do these people think they are?

He's ready to get out, when the receptionist comes up with a good idea. "Why not drive over to Cherry Creek after you've dropped Ms. Dexter off at the clinic?" she suggests. "There are some great restaurants and coffee places. And if you want to get something to read, the Tattered Cover is there too."

The bookstore suggestion resonates, not just with Grayson, but with Ros too. She tells him she doesn't want him to hang around.

Grayson turns to leave, but the receptionist insists on taking him through the program a second time. "When you drop Ms. Dexter off at the clinic, be sure to ask when she should be picked up. It'll probably take until five or so."

For lunch, he has an excellent Greek Salad with a glass of mediocre Burgundy. The ambiance in the small restaurant is pleasant, the lunch-time crowd less so. Grayson watches people's vacant faces and observes their eating habits. Some wolf their food down and leave, while others take their time. Almost everyone fiddles with an electronic device while chewing. Would anyone notice if he wore yellow shoes and a turquoise jacket? Not likely.

The old man at the pub in Boulder enters his thoughts. It takes him a moment to recall his name. Rich—that's what it was. Well, Rich didn't miss a beat. He'd have everyone here figured out in no time.

Outside, it should be cold. Early December gales should be lashing out at him, forcing him into the next doorway. Instead, a warm blanket of air smothers him.

He walks a block too far, soaking up the mid-day sun. At the Tattered Cover he ends up in the aisle that deals with parenting. He didn't look for it, but now that he's here he pulls several titles from their shelves. Maybe there's something that deals with his situation. Fathers and Sons. He vaguely remembers a book by that title—another Russian classic of which he can't recall the plot line.

After aimlessly looking at books and magazines, he leaves, thinking a cup of coffee would be nice. He knows there is a coffee shop inside the bookstore, but he first wants to kill some time. It's not even one thirty.

He's walked three blocks when he notices a Starbucks logo and then he sees Pereira. For a few seconds it's merely someone he recognizes. Then his brain links the stocky body and the pudgy face to the seer. Grayson surprises himself by remembering his name. Abelard Pereira.

Next, he sees that Pereira has spotted him, too. He walks up to the seer and greets him, holding out his hand. "Jack Grayson," he says. "I came to see you a few months ago."

"Ah, yes," Pereira replies thoughtfully, "I remember you now, Mr. Grayson."

"You helped me a lot. You opened my eyes to things I wasn't aware of."

Pereira looks up at him and, for a second or two, Grayson feels pressured to say more. Then he notices the seer's eyes: something isn't right with them. Pereira looks at Grayson's face, which is no more than two feet from his own, the way he'd look at a sunset across the sea. His eyes seem out of focus. Grayson remembers that gaze from his appointment.

"Mr. Pereira," he tries.

There is no sign that Pereira has heard him. Grayson feels uneasy and wonders if the seer will faint. He takes Pereira's arm and is surprised by how heavy it feels.

The trance ends, but not in the way Grayson thought. He watches Pereira's blurry eyes regain their focus, center on his face and then open wide.

"God!" the seer whispers, as if he'd seen something dreadful that he wants to communicate only to himself.

"Mr. Pereira, are you all right? I think you need to sit down."

The seer just looks at him, his plump face bluish-white now.

"Maybe we can go into the Starbucks together," Grayson tries.

Finally, Pereira manages to snap out of it. He firmly shakes his head, as if he'd caught a chill. Then he apologizes and hurriedly walks away.

Grayson can't figure out what happened. But he's certain that what he's just seen in the seer's eyes was a sadness deep enough to drown in.

WHEN GRAYSON JOGS DOWN THE ridge, he's surprised to see Ros sitting at the edge of the pond. She's crouched over a patch of reeds, dressed in her green warm-up suit. That was the color of the reeds and grasses not long ago, Grayson thinks. Now look at them, brittle and dull brown in the late autumn cold.

As he slows down to catch his breath, he notices that Ros is wearing far too little. He approaches her shouting jovially, "How about coming in with me and getting a jacket and a hat," and only when she turns her face up to him can he see that she's crying.

"Oh no, my sweet Ros, you need more than warm clothes," he says as he crouches down behind her and puts his arms around her cold shoulders. He kisses her hair. "How can I help?"

"Just be with me. Hold me."

As he puts his cheek next to hers, he notices the ancient-looking, ochre bug on her outstretched hand: the head seems to consist of only eyes and mouth, the six legs look spindly compared with the fat torso, and the two folded back wings are so tiny they look completely out of proportion. Ros must have caught it from between the reeds; it sits in a puddle of dirty water, seemingly at ease.

"What is it?" Grayson asks.

"It's a damselfly, I think."

"A damselfly?" Grayson is surprised but knows that Ros is the expert. "How come it's so different from the ones you sketch?"

"It's a nymph, Grayson. It's been born from a damselfly's eggs and next spring, or the one after, what you see will split apart and a damselfly will emerge from it." Ros says this in bits, fighting to get out the words and he holds her tighter. "Oh, Grayson. I was so excited when I found the first nymph last week." Her voice breaks and she starts to cry again. Grayson cradles her body and together they rock, until she continues. "Imagine, next spring's dragonflies or damsels right here, on our property, Grayson! It's all I could have dreamed of."

"You'll be here, Ros, to witness it," is all Grayson can think of saying.

"No. Now the nymphs will hatch when I'm gone," Ros gets out, before more sobs shake her.

Grayson has always thought of Ros as tough, but now her body feels as frail and defenceless as the frozen grasses lining the pond. All he knows to do is to keep rocking and tell her not to say such things, but to concentrate on wanting to be here at her pond come spring.

"I don't want to die, Grayson," she moans, and he promises her she will be here to tend her garden and sketch at her pond. *They* will be here together, he wanting to learn from her how damselflies hatch and how they fly along the shore and mate in mid-air. "We have to believe, Ros. We need to have faith."

While Grayson says that he thinks he wouldn't want to live without Ros. He would have coped with life had he never met her, but losing her would be too much to bear. And while he thinks that Ros dwells on the injustice of having been unloved so long and then finding the man who gives her what she needs and having to die.

They don't say anything for a long while. They just crouch together, surrounded by brittle, tired reeds whose stalks have started to break under the onslaught of frost and wind, Grayson cradling Ros' shivering body.

Later, he takes her by her hands and helps her up. She's wearing his fleece jacket as they walk off towards the ranch house, Grayson saying he'll make tea, or hot chocolate if she'd like that better.

SHE LOOKED FRAIL, GRAYSON THINKS as he drives home, this time without Ros. He wanted to stay at the hospital with her or, if that wasn't possible, overnight at a nearby hotel. But Ros insisted he drive home. "It'll give you something to do, Grayson. Something to take your mind off it."

For a while, the moon is on his left. It's not the embryonic sliver Ros saw not too long ago, not the moon of promise. This full moon droops hard and cold, like a pale lead ball threatening to crush Grayson and what is left of his pitiful life.

I'd rather be there with Ros, he thinks. Leaving was a mistake. He drives at a steady 50 miles, his thoughts dwelling on the light-blue gown and the plastic bracelet saying ROSALYN DEXTER on it, followed by a long number and a reference to her penicillin allergy. She was shivering before he left. He got the nurse to bring her a heated blanket.

When Grayson enters the house, he sees the frame with her portrait on the slim harvest table by the door. It's the picture he took on their camping trip. Her face is tanned and healthy, no sign of the sickness inside her, no possibility of viciously destructive cells recruiting others to join their ruinous cause.

He wonders what he'll do, then notices the red light flashing on his answering machine. He pushes the playback button and listens. First, Jeffrey Caldwell from the National Consumer Council soliciting a membership that entitles you to low-cost loans. Then his insurance company. Grayson thinks they've called to remind him to book his disability reassessment, but it's a solicitation. They want him to call in to discuss his home insurance needs. "Bastards!" he swears to himself. "They actually think they can sell me something while trying to take away my benefits." When he opens the lid to press ERASE, he notices how shaky his hand is.

Grayson remembers that he's still wearing his jacket and takes it off. Ros' windbreaker hangs from the pegboard and above it, on the shelf, is the baseball cap with the Aspen leaf that makes her look so good. He reaches up to it and closes his eyes and lets his fingertips rest on it for a few seconds.

"I don't want to lose you, Grayson," were the last words she said. He was amazed that even then, not knowing whether it would be their last time together, she called him Grayson. He held her tight for a long while, not wanting to let go and fighting back tears. She was wrapped in the hot blanket when he kissed her, his hands feeling the hot woollen cocoon and his lips meeting the cold, taut surface of hers. He kissed her on the forehead too and let his cheeks rest against her chilled face. And then he turned to leave, awkwardly pacing backward so that he could hold her in his eyes as long as possible.

I don't want to lose you, Grayson.

He's afraid. When Ros came out of the pre-op procedure and he saw that bracelet, an image of her arm dangling lifelessly from under a sheet flashed through his mind.

At a quarter past midnight Grayson sits in the easy chair, trying to read. While looking at letters and lines, he hears the nurse at the operating station telling him that it would be a long procedure. They'd start at five a.m. and if he phoned in around eleven, they'd be able to tell him more.

Things Kepperling explained come floating through Grayson's consciousness. He sees the white fine-boned fingers with the red marker drawing a dotted line showing where the skull would be opened. Then the steady, low voice, mechanically describing the removal of the tumor. The word CRANIOTOMY echoes through the caverns of Grayson's mind.

Later, the surgeon's fingers again, this time pushing the X-ray toward them, the menacing dark spot much larger than Grayson had imagined. He feels Ros' hand inside his own tense up. And finally, Grayson hears the surgeon explain the risks: which parts of the brain are endangered by the procedure itself and what will happen if things go wrong. Then Kepperling sits back in his chair and inquires if there are questions, like the general manager of a bank asking his branch heads whether they have questions about the latest fee increase. He doesn't seek Ros' eyes, asking "Do you have any questions, Ms. Dexter?" He looks at his desk instead, contemplates the dreaded X-ray image and says, "Are there any questions?"

Grayson groans as he watches Ros, sees the single tear leave her eye and make its way to the corner of her mouth. She clears her throat and when she says it her voice is clear and determined. "What are my chances of survival?"

Grayson's gaze turns back to the doctor and as he sees his expression his distress grows. Kepperling shoots his patient a look that says your question is unexpected, pauses long enough to appear dignified and finally responds. "Fifty percent."

Grayson relives the last moments of the interview. The discussion about the alternatives leaves him in tatters. There are none, Kepperling says, other than for the tumor to grow larger and slowly strangle the brain's functions. Given where it's located, Ros' sight could be first to go. He places a sheaf of forms in front of Ros, mutters something about the hospital's need to be exempted from liability and holds out a leaky ballpoint pen. His pale fingers are smudged with black ink.

Grayson relives these scenes once or twice in the right sequence, then bits of his recollections reappear randomly as he nods off.

In his dream, he walks across a frost-covered lawn. He can hear his steps. There's an unfriendly crunch each time he sets a foot down. Grayson is headed toward a pedestrian crossing that leads to the hospital lot where he's parked his car. When he gets there, he looks up at the light and for a moment he's confused because everything has turned black and white. He asks himself how he'll know which color is which, but it only takes him a second to figure it out. Since everyone else is waiting, the light must be red—all he has to do is wait for it to change.

When that happens Grayson steps out onto the crosswalk. Someone behind him yells. He turns his head to see why and that makes things worse, because if he'd looked the other way he would have seen the vehicle that was about to strike him and could have sidestepped it.

The bang is like a distant explosion, slowed down by some tech kid in a sophisticated sound studio so that it lasts forever. When eventually it stops he can hear the voices. His eyes are still closed, but he can tell they belong to people discussing an event that's terrified and yet thrilled them. And then their chatter grows faint and the white background noise that never leaves the city fades out too.

In the ambulance Grayson sees two blurred figures hovering over him. Someone in the background yells. He wants to escape, but crippling pain prevents him. He wonders why the only people with him are the medics. Marlene. Why is she not here, or the boys? He thinks of Samantha, too, probably off in some distant ashram, blissfully ignorant of what's just happened to him. He remembers the rusty platter of a sun on the postcard and the lone plow man in the foreground.

And Ros, where is my sweet Ros? The skeletons of my past, he ruminates, only to realize that Ros is not that, not a skeleton. Not yet. I should be with Ros, not she here, he grasps, and then his thoughts turn to panic as he comprehends that no one will look after Ros now.

The piercing wail of the siren comes on again and he's tempted to let himself slip back into painless nothingness. But he fights the urge to do so, realizing he must be there for Ros. He shoots up from his recliner, relieved that he's been dreaming, but an instant later panicking, as he realizes the operation is not part of his dream world.

He looks at the clock on the kitchen wall and sees that it's four thirty a.m. Another half hour before it begins.

His mouth feels dry. He gets up and stretches and walks around the house, hearing her voice, *I don't want to lose you, Grayson,* and responding, I don't want to lose you either. He ends up in the bedroom, lifts one of Ros' sweaters to his face and inhales deeply.

He cries.

Later he picks himself up and walks to the kitchen where he pours himself a cognac. He gulps it down in one swallow and convinces himself he's feeling better. He pours another and takes his glass and walks to the front door to go outside.

His boots are neatly placed at the entrance, but putting them on seems too damn trivial. In his slippers Grayson walks to the fence between the driveway and the field and stands in the night. The moon is smaller now that it's risen halfway toward its zenith, but much brighter. Grayson thinks of the times he's stood here with Ros, looking up into the night sky and he feels lonelier than ever. He can't wait to have her back, yet he no longer thinks it will happen. By now they must be getting ready. He's hoping they're behind schedule.

Back inside the kitchen he grabs the cognac bottle for another refill, then puts it down and pushes it to the back of the counter. He pours tap water into the round glass instead and wanders over to his office. His computer is on. The screensaver, one of Ros' fall shots of aspens, fills the dark room with a yellowish hue. Grayson sits down and stares at the monitor, unfocused. What if she doesn't come back? Heaviness settles on his chest; he doesn't think he'll want to go on. He wonders how he'd do it. In a hot bath with a plastic bag over his head, maybe. Then he remembers the package in the safe.

He goes downstairs to the den and opens the mirrored sliding door behind which the floor-safe is mounted. But when he fiddles with the dial he realizes that he can't remember the combination. He's almost relieved that he has to go back to his computer to check it. Each small task kills a few more minutes.

Next, he wonders whether he shouldn't instead wish for

time to move slowly. Every minute is a minute of life for Ros, he reminds himself. Provided you can call it living when you get your skull cut up. The thought brings tears to his eyes.

When the safe is finally open, he removes a bunch of thick envelopes and taped-up file folders. He reaches all the way in and pulls out the white cardboard box. A green string keeps it shut and there's a slipknot on top. He's never given the string any thought but now he does. It's the same twine he found everywhere in his parents' garden, tying roses to the sides of arbors and holding hollyhocks to their stakes.

He could pull the knot or yank at the twine and break it, but Grayson takes the package upstairs, carrying it as if it were of inestimable value or posed grave danger. An altar boy entrusted with a sacred object by his priest. Or a soldier carrying a landmine yet to be defused.

Standing at the kitchen counter, he grabs a paring knife and slices through the twine on either side of the knot, before lifting the top off and reaching in. The bundle of stained beige terry cloth is heavy. He holds it in both hands, weighing the Enfield service revolver inside the way his father used to. He remembers the big fleshy hands and the smell of gun oil and hears the voice. "Do you want to feel it, Jack?"

The weight surprises him.

"Did grandpa shoot people with it, Dad?"

"No, Jack. He was a major. Senior officers don't get to shoot at the enemy too often. And this thing is notoriously inaccurate. But it was more precious to him than anything. So precious he broke the law for it."

"How did he break the law?"

"He didn't return it. Couldn't do it, after carrying it through half of Italy to help win the war. So he told them it had been stolen."

Grayson remembers asking whether grandpa had ever explained what it was like, being in a war, and stopping in mid-sentence, terrified by the hardening of his father's steely eyes and the twitch under his eye. "No need to know. Not for you, Jack. Grandpa was in Europe and I served in Korea. You'll be doing it the easy way, going to university, so you'll never serve your country the way we did."

Grayson feels anger rise in him. Wanting him to take over the damned dealership, but resentful that Jack wasn't a soldier like he and his grandfather had once been. "What did you expect me to do, moron?" he mutters to himself as he puts the gun back into the box. "Start a fucking war, so you could delude yourself into believing that your son fought for yet another good cause?"

Grayson turns on the tap and holds his glass under it. He's thirsty. He can't remember ever being this thirsty.

GRAYSON KEEPS STUMBLING, THE TIPS of his feet catching furrows that are impossible to see. Still, he keeps running at a good clip. Clouds are obscuring the moon now, drizzling half frozen bits of rain on him. He knows they've started the operation. He can tell.

He imagines the saw cutting through Ros' skull and bits of blood welling to the surface and mixing with ground specks of bone, before being removed by some suction device. He wonders whether blood and sawdust and remnants of discarded artery from one patient are pooled with those of others, ending up in larger and larger containers. What do they do with that stuff, his mind asks and he gets disgusted with the idea and with himself and feels badly about thinking this way.

Then he falls and one of his knees smacks into the ground hard and his hands feel the raspy surface of the soil and Grayson realizes how cold it must be and yet how hot his body is. Like embers!

As he struggles back onto his feet, his father's face is in front of him again, as it has been in the kitchen when he looked at the Enfield. The grey eyes are following him, cruel and relentless in their intensity. And the twitch. Every time Grayson allows himself to look there is the fucking twitch, arcing from his father's eye down to the corner of his mouth, its quickening pace foreshadowing trouble.

Grayson runs. He wants to banish his father, purge him forever, and yet he comprehends it's not what he should do, not what Hendrick or Ros would have suggested.

The images come at an even faster rate now, each like a blow across his back, making it impossible for him to allow them in, let alone welcome them. Instead, he runs ever harder to escape the memories, convinced that the more he pushes himself, the better his chance of drowning out the agony. And if he runs far enough he'll escape it altogether. Running has helped before, something inside him says.

But the celluloid bits of his father keep coming at him. Ignoring Jack at the breakfast table, sneering at him in the den, telling him to get out of the garage. And then the scene Grayson dreads more than all others. His father behind his enormous desk at the dealership and Marlene and he standing on the other side.

Grayson looks at Marlene's face and sees shame in it, as though she had disgraced herself, and that emboldens him to take her hand and speak up. Now the twitch again, faster this time, and eyes like blue ice. The mouth quivering for an instant, then calling Marlene an opportunist lusting after their money.

Grayson comes to the end of the field, his legs steel and his lungs capable of anything. He runs, down the hollow and up the side of the ridge, like he does every morning, but this is night and Ros is in hospital and he's having a date with his cursed, no-good, fucking sham of a father.

Halfway up the ridge he hears him yell, "Then get out, you failure of a son. Take your white trash whore with you and don't ever come back!"

He remembers being on the run then too, cradling Marlene

in his arms and giving her shelter while finishing university, and working nights as a room boy at the Sheraton, and later giving her dignity and pride in what they built together. Yes, he ran then too. Never to return.

A branch hits him in the face, cutting his cheek and lip, and Grayson falls again. He tastes blood and lies there, seeing nothing in the black forest except the faint outline of the heavy trunk under which he's come to rest and the edges of a canopy of branches.

He gasps for air, fearing his nostrils will breathe in the smell of gasoline instead and then he knows his lungs could cope even with that, at least this one time. In the distance, he hears a phone ring and then the ringing gets louder until it's right inside his brain, so piercing it threatens to split his skull. Next comes the voice of his parents' doctor, telling him how sorry he is that his mother has passed, the words spoken with well-practiced calm and solemnity. Grayson follows the conversation with the doctor but grows impatient with it, wanting to go back to his father and the anger that's been with him all these years and he wants to let its dark mantle soothe him. The bastard's ruined my life for too long, he fumes, and he feels good and righteous.

The doctor says, "Mr. Grayson, I have to bring up the subject of your Dad." And Grayson grows angrier yet, realizing he's being asked to help, and he listens on as the doctor explains about his father being alone in his tower, half-insane and living off root beer and cookies and a nurse coming by twice a day to check on him and take him to the bathroom.

Grayson starts to grab at the wet forest floor, feeling twigs and pine cones and sticky things, and he cries in big, violent sobs, cries not because he feels sorry for his deranged father but because he's reliving his struggle. He remembers deciding to withdraw the nursing service and let the bastard slowly rot in his fucking tower, and if he didn't rot he'd drown in the shit of his cookies!

He claws at the soil, feeling its loose, wet surface and the icy hardness underneath and he feels shame that he didn't have the capacity to help. His tears run freely now and eventually the sobs stop, too, and all that's left is surrender to the pain that is below the anger, and then there are tears of a different kind.

He reaches forward and pulls himself up toward the trunk, his fingers digging in as far as they can go and his arms pulling the weight of his body behind them. When he gets to the trunk he hugs it and holds onto it hard, ends of broken-off branches pushing into the side of his chest and cutting his neck.

He keeps crying, remembering the final visit to his father and smelling the stench of sickness and age all over. He hears himself say that he'll sell the house, his voice haughty and self-righteous, and then he remembers the satisfaction he felt each month when paying the invoice from the nursing home saying BASIC SERVICE on it. And finally he lives through the call which tells him of his father's death and his decision not to go to the funeral.

His sobs intensify again and he holds onto the tree with all his might, as he realizes how hard Ros has tried to help him get this out and that now she'll probably never know. He pushes his cheek into the hard bark, feeling worse than he has in his whole life, even worse than when his father turned him away and called Marlene a whore and worse than when he was in the wheelchair. And that is when he grasps the depth of Hendrick's wisdom—things can't get worse than this, they just can't. He may as well let it in, allow his father's arrogance and cruelty and selfishness to dwell. It's been there anyway: the nervous tick, the pitiless ice-blue eyes, the

Enfield, the heartless language designed to crush. Except it's been buried, its attempts to unearth itself tormenting him day after day, and now it's there to be felt, experienced with all his senses, allowed to exist as his past.

Grayson still cries when he lets himself slide onto his back to rest. He notices how itchy his eyes are and how new tears keep welling up, even though he no longer wants to cry. He feels cold too. When he finally gets on his knees and looks at the tree above him the first traces of light are showing through the branches.

Later, in the shower, Grayson turns on the water and lets it heat up, before stepping under it. He cranes his neck, lets the stream of water hit his face, breathes in the moisture. The frozen fields and his tree are gone from his mind, but his father is not. Dozens of images crowd in on him.

"Over here, Jack," his father calls and Grayson sees his dad in the new car, behind the rolled down window, motioning him to hop in. It's a spring day and he wanted to play with the others on the way home, but having his father come to pick him up is that much better. He's immensely pleased.

Other recollections rush by. They're at the zoo, they're playing with model cars he's brought home from the dealership, and then they're standing in the kitchen, just the two of them. Grayson is no more than four feet tall, his Dad towering above him, exuding strength and wisdom. Dad announces they'll make scrambled eggs and demonstrably holds up the carton, then inexplicably drops it. Egg is running down the fridge door, bits of yellow cling to dad's shoes and pant cuffs, and an ocean of liquid sits on the floor. Dad asks him to get a rag and when he comes running back,

Jack slips on the gooey mess and slides across the kitchen floor. Now his pyjamas are soiled, too. He looks up at his Dad, a bit afraid because Dad looks down at him gravely, but then Dad starts laughing and gets down on the floor too and they both laugh for a long time, as though nothing in the world could be funnier than breaking a dozen eggs.

Grayson clings to the memory as he steps out of the shower and starts drying himself. He doesn't know it, but he smiles.

Then he sees the blood on the towel and that reminds him of the time when his little sister died. He realizes it's a memory that's been suppressed forever; he can't even recall what she looked like. She was less than a year old when it happened.

Grayson remembers how hurt his mother was when Dad blamed her and how much he wished to help. But his mother stayed in her room for weeks and didn't want him near her. Only his Dad was allowed in.

The white towel is soiled with red streaks and when Grayson looks at the mirror he sees how messed up his face and neck are. He takes sterile gauze and hydrogen peroxide from under the sink and starts dabbing at the blood. The cuts are deep but they'll heal.

GRAYSON SETS HIS ALARM; HE gives himself two and a half hours. He's asleep almost immediately.

When he wakes he feels unexpectedly rested, but the ordeal of a few hours ago snaps back to his consciousness before he's on his feet. He remembers the image of his cut-up face and neck and walks straight to the mirror to see if his recollection is accurate. When he sees the crusted blood, he thinks of Ros and feels anxiety. Christ, what if she's dead? His pulse quickens and he has trouble breathing properly. He rushes to the kitchen and leans against the edge of the counter. It helps.

Later, with a mug of steaming coffee in his hand, he walks to the door and opens it. The field stretches out before him, fragile sheets of frozen drizzle showing pure and perfect against the broken soil, and Grayson remembers they weren't there yet when he stumbled through the dark of the night. The ridge looks high in the morning light and Grayson finds it hard to believe that he's been up there. The pines are dusted white, which gives them a look of serenity and make it seem unlikely that they've witnessed such drama just hours ago.

The cold reminds Grayson that he's dressed in nothing more than the sweatshirt he slept in. He has a glimpse into a future without Ros, where he walks around in his pyjama top all day, unmotivated to dress or shave or shower, dishes piling up in the sink and dust balls floating around the house. A voice inside him says no—he's gone through tragedy before and pulled himself together. Remember the wheelchair, Grayson. You pulled yourself up and walked again, became a skier and a jogger. Another voice responds, that's why I can't do it again. How many times can you push me down and expect me to get up again?

He walks back to the kitchen and pours himself a glass of water. Then he sees the cognac bottle and takes a gulp from that. He feels the sting of salt on his scratched up cheek and realizes that he's been crying again. Crying is becoming a constant. He lifts the bottle to his lips and takes another swig.

He takes a quick shower, making sure his face doesn't get wet. The cuts and abrasions have dried a bit; keeping them dry will help them heal. In the mirror he notices his stubble.

At nine thirty he phones the number he's been given.

"Let me see, Mr. Grayson," the station nurse says. And after checking, "Miss Dexter's operation is taking longer than expected, so there's no rush for you to get here."

"Last night they said I should be there around eleven."

"Let's see, you live in Evergreen, right? Why don't you call me again at noon? I should have an update by then. And if anything changes I'll call you, okay?"

He asks for her name. Beth Venerosa.

As soon as he hangs up he thinks of questions he should have asked. His anxiety returns. Why are they taking longer? He lets himself slump into his easy chair and concentrates on his breathing, but after consciously inhaling a dozen times he forgets again.

Grayson thinks he should dress and go for a walk, but he can't take the risk of being out. They might call him. He considers meditating, but knows he can't do it. The onslaught of fear and frustration is inescapable.

At noon he's on the phone with Beth again. She tells him it may take even longer than they'd earlier thought. Grayson asks whether there are complications.

"We don't get details at our station, but we do know that neurosurgical procedures are often unpredictable."

Grayson's heart sinks. "What do you suggest I do?"

"Whatever feels right, Mr. Grayson, but there is no point in you being here before three. Come to the 4th floor west station and ask for me. That's where the recovery area is. And you may want to bring a book with you."

He thanks Beth and hangs up. Then he realizes how hungry he is.

On the kitchen counter is the box, just the way he left it last night, its top and the scrunched-up green twine to the side of it. Inside, resting on the cloth rests the Enfield, benign and inconsequential now. Something to be disposed of. Grayson still sees his father's eyes when he looks at the gun, but the anger is gone. What's left is a yawning sadness he knows will always be there.

THE CORRIDORS ARE DEPRESSING: GREYISH mauve, greyish green, plain grey. And the smell. Faint at first, then stinging his nostrils. As Jack Grayson turns the corner, he sees the Latino janitor mopping the floor. Ammonia. The bank of neon lighting points him onward, stark and unimaginative like the centre line painted on a highway.

On Grayson's right are doors with tiny pieces of glass inserted, allowing a glimpse inside the numbered rooms. Grayson looks through one of the windows, but all he can see is a dividing wall blocking the view to the beds. He wonders who designs hospitals. Some politician's nephew, probably. The same guy who's in charge of the blueprints for prisons.

To the left is the building's outside wall. Here the windows have been placed too high up on the wall and are too narrow to let in sufficient light. What are they afraid of, he muses. Patients taking their lives before the surgeons can get at them? Grayson concludes it's the visitors they're concerned with. Visitors unable to bear the misery their loved ones are reduced to, fleeing the sterility and hopelessness of it all.

Two nurses come through the set of swinging doors in the distance, carrying paper coffee cups and chatting. Grayson walks up to them and asks where the recovery station is. They hesitate, then say, "Straight through the doors to your right." My cuts and my stubble, Grayson remembers.

At the station he asks for Beth. When she comes around the corner he pre-empts her question by saying, "I know I look like an escaped convict."

"Maybe you should have your face looked at, while you're here, Mr. Grayson. Are you all right?"

He ignores the suggestion and asks, "How is Ros?"

Beth says she'll check on her progress and disappears around the wall of a workstation. Grayson looks at the stacks of papers that cover every surface and wonders how often patients get mixed up.

When Beth comes back she says she can't tell him anything new. They're still operating.

"Is everything okay?" Grayson tries, his throat feeling incredibly dry.

"I can't tell you more, Mr. Grayson." She looks at him compassionately. "A craniotomy is a difficult procedure."

"You can't tell me…" Grayson repeats.

"No, I'm afraid I can't. The best I can do is tell you where you can get a good cup of coffee and sit comfortably."

Grayson wants to say, Ros made me coffees, cappuccinos actually, but he feels the tears coming back and all he manages to say while turning away is, "Thank you."

He hears Beth tell him to be back in an hour.

The main floor cafeteria reminds him of an airport. Rows of colorful, fused-together metal seats along the walls, with metal tables and metal chairs in between. Everything bolted to the floor, as if hospital patients or their visitors were skilled furniture thieves. Overhead, every thirty feet or so, a TV monitor flickers. From where he stands, Grayson can see some general standing at a lectern, a roomful of reporters shooting questions at him. Syria, he assumes. Or maybe Afghanistan. They're at it again.

Grayson lines up. He doesn't want to look at the screens, but the bits of sound that reach him lure him back. By the time he orders his coffee a commercial is running. An elderly woman in a spring meadow, pretty hair but her teeth a bit too white. They're selling drugs, Grayson registers. Next, they'll go through the warnings: take it and liver cancer, infertility or prostate enlargement may be yours.

He picks a table that's equally far removed from two TV sets and stretches his bad leg. It's been throbbing since he left home. He sips the coffee and is surprised by how good it tastes; strong, the way he likes it. And not boiling hot.

He stares at the line-up at the food counter and thinks of how Ros always knew how much more there was to his father. She knew right away, even before they became lovers. But he never talked to her about it. About Marlene and the boys, yes, and about Samantha, occasionally. And as she got more involved in meditation she got curious about Hendrick. The Fedex driver, the parking lot attendant, and Grayson's smugness and insensitivity—all that came out, and once it was out they touched on it again and again and it was okay.

But not his father, and now he knows why he stayed away from the subject. Now that Ros is somewhere up there, her skull open like a coffee mug, with strangers poking around inside—now he knows and he can't go and tell her, for Christ's sake!

Grayson notices the blood on his finger and licks it away. He lightly touches his cheek and inspects his finger and it's smeared again. Then he takes a napkin from the container on the table and dabs his cut. He has to stop picking at it.

His eyes are staring at the people coming and going, but his brain doesn't register what he sees; his mind has turned back to his father. Grayson is surprised that in his thoughts he is now a child. He's noticed that first while driving to the hospital. He is a child and his Dad is all-knowing and strong. He feels shielded by Dad's raw, masculine power. The memories of later, when things start going wrong are there too, but they're no longer alone. Other childhood recollections are competing for attention and Grayson is happy to see that they bring images of contentment and joy. He wonders if they'll be strong enough one day to conquer the resentment he knows is still inside him.

And then he remembers Ros saying that she wants him to think good thoughts while she's under, good thoughts only, and he feels terrible because he's forgotten about that. Here is Ros, he thinks, my constant rescuer, my nurturer. And in the end, I can't even do that for her: think good thoughts.

He closes his eyes and shuts out the people and the noises which engulf him and concentrates on his breathing and thinks of Ros. He thinks of her behind the counter at the café, pistons hissing and steam blowing and she looking at him in her no-nonsense Aussie kind of way, shouting, "Your usual"?

That was before he knew much about her. Now he knows her body and her soul and he loves what he knows. So much so that he wants to be with her always. Help me get Ros back, he prays, and he can feel the moisture trickle down his cheeks again and pinch his bleeding wound and then blood and salt reach the corner of his mouth. He pushes his tongue there, not sure whether he's doing so to taste it or to make it disappear. Give me Ros back, please!

He hears Ros' voice again, saying he has to think good things and he ponders what those are, good things, and decides he'll think of Ros in her favorite places. Her barn, light streaming in through the skylights and Ros standing there in front of her taped-up proofs, studying the colors that are there and the possibility of new ones she could create. Or Ros kneeling in the moist black top soil of her new garden covering plants with mulch for the winter, and then coming back into the house, chilled to the bone, and Grayson putting on tea, and while it's boiling holding her tightly, rubbing her arms and her back. Yes, this is what Ros wanted me to think. Good thoughts. Thoughts of love. Thoughts that heal.

His tears are running freely. He asks himself how much is in there, in those tear ducts, and then he considers the people standing and sitting around him. They probably think he's crying because someone close to him has died. But that's not how it works. If he went up now and they told him Ros was dead and showed him her lifeless body, her arm with the plastic bracelet hanging down over the side of the bed, he couldn't cry. There'd be nothing left inside him, no tears, no sobs, no energy—only the weight and futility of bottomless, black grief.

Grayson opens his eyes and, yes, there are people who're staring at him, and as his eyes meet theirs they hurriedly look away. He takes another napkin and wipes his eyes and pats his cheek and then reaches for the coffee which has turned cold.

Nearly an hour has passed. He wanders toward the elevator. He stands against the wall and closes his eyes and does as he did a few minutes ago, thinks of Ros, this time on their camping trip. He stands high up on a knoll and hollers to Ros and she waves back from outside their tent and he swears he can see the radiance of her eyes against her tanned face.

"Please give her back to me," he whispers to himself. "Nothing else matters. Nothing." And as he ponders these words he knows that he's moved on to a new part of his life and hope fills him. Never mind rebuilding his lost past—Martin and Oliver will find their own way and neither Marlene nor Samantha need him. But Ros does. He has to be there for her. Nothing matters except Ros being alive now, and he being with her.

He hears someone ask if he's okay and as he opens his eyes he sees the hospital employee dressed in green, an uneasy looking young woman who must have thought he was dizzy, leaning against the wall like that. Grayson thanks her, assures her he's all right.

Inside the elevator he closes his eyes again and this time he thinks of Ros sitting in the sand, her legs crossed. To her side is the hut with the crudely painted shutters and behind her the turquoise of the ocean, unreal in its intensity.

When the elevator stops, he looks down the long corridor and starts walking, unaware now of the misplaced, overly narrow windows and the wretched color scheme, his mind firmly on Ros. And when he comes around the corner where the janitor was, the smell of ammonia is gone and the bank of neon seems less menacing. He dwells on his good thoughts of Ros when he goes through the swinging doors and stops doing so only when he comes to the recovery station and sees Beth.

She smiles. "You can go down to 416A, Mr. Grayson. She's still under anaesthesia and it may be a while before she comes to."

"She's okay, then?"

"It's been a long operation. Be very gentle with her. She'll be exhausted."

Grayson turns down the corridor, counting the room numbers. He passes two bathrooms and then sees the number, painted white on the metal-framed double door. He stands for a few moments before entering.

THE FIRST THING HE NOTICES when he sees Ros is how pale she is. Her skin looks like delicate porcelain. Not white or beige or any definable shade. Colorless. Almost transparent.

He looks at the bandage and wonders how they got all her hair under it, before realizing that they must have shaved it off. And then he notices a slight movement in her arm and he knows she's alive and his tear ducts open again, releasing silent floods. He keeps looking for more signs of life, focusing first on her arms and the tubes coming out of her wrists. He studies her face, oddly different than it was before. White gauze covers most of her forehead and an oxygen tube reaches into her nose. They've done things to her, but still, it's his Ros. God has given him his Ros back!

He takes a chair from the corner and puts it next to the bed and stares. He doesn't want to miss anything, not the slightest twitch of her nostrils or quiver of her pale lips. Grayson considers touching her hands, ever so gently, but he decides against it, thinking he should let her wake up by herself. Instead he talks to her, moving his lips without a sound, knowing she will not hear it but certain that it will reach her anyway.

He tells her about the good thoughts first. Standing in the barn looking at the colors on her palette, shafts of light above her.

Kneeling in the garden and at the edge of her pond. And the two of them camping, strong and tanned in the summer light.

A nurse comes and checks the monitors behind Ros and asks Grayson if Ros has opened her eyes yet. When he shakes his head she says she'll check again in a few minutes.

Grayson is glad when the nurse is gone. He feels so close to Ros now, closer than ever, and that makes him imagine her body against his. And as he does so exhaustion overcomes him and he dozes off.

Next, the sun floods the room and Grayson feels the heat rise and that wakes him. Ros' eyes are open now and her teeth show and she says, "Grayson," and then falls back asleep. She looks even paler than before.

He reaches for her hands, placing his flatly over the tubes that run across them. They feel cold and he thinks, I have to make my warmth flow into her, and he concentrates on doing that until she opens her eyes again.

This time Ros says, "Your face." The two syllables are so faint he isn't sure he's heard them or read her lips. Her eyes close again and Grayson isn't sure whether she's gone back to sleep. He says, "I'm so happy to have you back," a bit louder now and he can tell Ros hears him, because this time her lips part as if into a smile, and so he says it again. Then he adds, "Only you matter now, Ros. Only you."

He has so much to tell her; the past twenty-four hours seem like an eternity. But first Ros has to get her strength back.

His hand is stroking her porcelain cheek, as Grayson thinks of the two of them walking in the park outside. The windows are too high for him to see out, but he knows it's down there.

Once in the park they'll look for a bench where they can sit quietly, like the one in Aspen by the river. They'll have to pick a sunny day. With her being so weak, they can't take chances. Lightly cupping Ros' hand with his own, Grayson nods off.

As always, his dream starts with the closing of the polished stainless steel doors. The elevator takes its time as it usually does and he doesn't mind. And when it stops on 34, the Fedex man steps in. Grayson expected this much. But there is to be no parking lot this time, no sweet spot and no gas gauge telling him to stop. No shooting and no looking from the outside in, either. This time, Grayson never gets past the Fedex man.

He hears Ros' voice next to him, asking, "I wonder who he really is, the Fedex guy." Grayson bristles at her intrusion, thinking she has no right to say that. And how could she talk, anyway, being dead? A crippling heaviness comes over him as he contemplates that fact and he feels his stomach and his throat tighten. He's almost relieved when he hears Ros' voice again, saying the same words and then repeating them over and over like a vinyl recording with a crack in it. "I wonder who he really is, the Fedex guy."

If there is nothing else left of Ros, at least I have her voice, he consoles himself. And then he finally pays attention to her words and thinks, Yeah, who the hell is he—I've always wanted to know. He remembers studying the Fedex man before and he does that again, starting with the wavy silver hair and the bronzed neck, slightly wrinkled but muscular—the neck of a man in his prime. He looks at the well-defined jaw line and sees this is a man of character. Grayson lets his eyes run along the powerful shoulder hidden under the blue twill of the uniform jacket and down the arm to where he knows the Fedex man's hand holds on to his envelope. He looks at the healthy thumb pressing against the envelope, studying the perfectly groomed nail and the smooth cuticle. A man of culture too.

And then Grayson raises his eyes again, hoping to steal a glimpse of his face, but it's invisible. All he can see is hair and below it an outline of forehead, a temple, a flawlessly shaped ear, its ridge even more darkly tanned than the neck joining it. Grayson decides to talk to the man, but his words have no sound. The only evidence that he's spoken is an achy dryness in his throat and the lingering memory of the nerves in his twitching lips.

Grayson considers his options and next decides to will the Fedex man to turn. He strains so hard he feels the dome of his head open and he can tell something far larger than a mere thought sallies forth, but again the Fedex man doesn't respond.

Grayson closes his eyes, because there is no point in keeping them trained on the stranger in front of him. He starts articulating his experience to himself. I'm failing, he thinks. I'm left without a way out once again.

He reminds himself of what will follow. First he'll feel sorry for himself, then there will be anger. But as he visualizes the liquid black anger flooding the caverns of his mind and then oozing down through his body the way ink seeps through the fibres of a blotter, an inspiration displaces these images. I don't want anger any more, he suddenly knows, and he feels unexpectedly liberated just thinking that. And as that happens there's a craving of such magnitude that for an instant he's afraid of it, much like a parched tree in the desert shivers when the first gust of wind reveals the advent of rain. But soon after the tree tastes its first drop it wants to soak up the sky and so it is with Grayson.

Give me acceptance instead, he thinks, a little cautious at first. But as his soul opens to the possibility of acceptance he invites it in enthusiastically, and moments later he's willing to surrender all that he is and he has and believes in—all that in exchange for the embrace of acceptance. He can feel the identities he held melt away. Grayson the father and the husband, Grayson the businessman and Grayson the victim, too—all dissolving like wisps of a dispersed cloud that only hours before seemed capable of bringing flood and destruction. And as the false Graysons he's created through his life disband another takes their place, one that's always been there but that he's forgotten about—the Grayson that's his essence. For an instant, he grasps all that and then it slips away again and he longs to regain the understanding he just had and the unforeseen bliss it brought him.

He opens his eyes again, this time with the anticipation of seeing a new world. A different elevator cab, perhaps, or a Fedex man who's not a stranger to him and on whom he can set eyes without apprehension.

A different reality reveals itself. The Fedex man slowly turns his face and an instant later he looks directly at Grayson, their two faces now a mere foot apart. And what Grayson sees is beautiful and terrible at the same time.

The Fedex man's face is that of his father, dark and menacing at first and then as radiant and joyful as it was when they cleaned broken eggs off the kitchen floor. But as the memory of that weekend morning takes hold, his father's face is already changing and now the expression is that of the gunman, mouth tense and brow creased with irritation. Martin is next and Grayson gets to see discomfort in his son's eyes, and then comes Oliver, not quite knowing what has happened between his father and nurse Celia, but afraid nonetheless.

The stranger's face changes features and expressions again: his mother is there, surprisingly with a smile on her face. And then a dozen and a hundred more faces appear. There's beautiful Ros and compassionate Sharon Bailey and Hegedus' wisdom and Samantha's innocence. The faces keep coming and give Grayson a million glances into the life he's lived, and in the end he understands—what he sees is the face of the Universe itself. A face that has to express every living thing, reflect every experience and manifest every possibility, because the Universe could not be perfect and all-knowing if it didn't do that.

As Grayson gains this insight the face before him becomes his own, and all the cruelties and mercies and hopes and despairs, the hurts and delights and the potential and inertia that reside in him are visible all at once. He observes flickers of anger and sparkles of unconditional love, sputters of fear and flashes of courage and he knows he is the Universe and the Universe is he, and he's mesmerized, awed and enchanted by this face as he watches its countless devilish and divine manifestations and keeps watching until the images all blur into one again, and that one is the image of acceptance and the changeless undying peace it brings.

Grayson contemplates that one face for a long time and as he does so, all emotions take flight and a sensation of great joy overcomes him, joy that he can finally see. Then there are tears and these are bittersweet. He weeps for the wasted years of judgment and hatred and anger and fear, and he cries with relief that all that is now unnecessary. And on the heels of his tears come happiness and laughter. Grayson laughs like he's never laughed before because he understands how simple everything was all along and how complicated he's made it.

Later yet, he starts feeling the peace he saw on the face of the Universe which was also his face. It touches him gently, that peace, and then engulfs him, bringing every cell of his body to a state of complete awareness. He could do everything now, from this position of peace, but it's not necessary to do anything. He lets himself slide onto his back tenderly and before he knows it he floats. The liquid under him is deliciously warm and it carries him.

He wonders what it is, this liquid, but he doesn't really care. What he knows is that all is well now, not only with him but with all. He's floating on the pool of universal consciousness itself. ❏

Notes and Acknowledgements

The Sweet Spot is my tenth book and my second novel. I wrote it in Toronto and Snowmass Village, Aspen's neighbouring town, although the first outline was conceived in a hammock outside Tulum, on Mexico's Caribbean coast in 2003. A final draft was completed in the fall of 2007.

All aspects of this book are fictional. Writing a novel about the human condition that is not strongly plot-driven was a challenge. Worse, I never had a pre-conceived notion of who the real Jack Grayson was or how he would navigate the obstacles that would characterize his journey. Nor did I have a clear vision of how the story-line might evolve. Thus, both the main character and the narrative simply evolved, a development that was not always easy for me to accept.

It took me a while to realize what my problem was: unlike Jack Grayson, I had never really suffered. Each novel causes its author to embark on a moral odyssey, and mine took me through numerous medical works, to the Book of Job, and finally to the sister I grew up with, Gaby.

Throughout her short life, Gaby had suffered, and only by opening myself to her agony did I finally get into Grayson's mind. And then, just when my novel was ready for submission to the publisher, Krista tragically died.

The loss of our daughter opened the floodgates to years of self-reflection. Keeping our family together and making sure Krista's three-year-old son Cameron would be well took precedence. Then came a long period of healing, during which nature walks, growing flowers, splitting wood at the cottage and the odd trip filled my free time. It's where I wanted to be.

Once I returned to writing, I embarked on a journey of self-therapy, reliving my life through a three-volume retrospective. That's why, for many years, my manuscript for this novel lay in a drawer, waiting to be rediscovered.

I'd like to thank all early readers for their comments that covered topics as diverse as gardening, biology and meditation practices, as well as the psychological and medical challenges associated with the recovery from severe trauma: Pamela Wilson, Michael Regan, James Weaver, Kristen Maire, Stephanie Rayner and Clare Pace. Fellow author Larry Gaudet was there to read my novel at various stages and Sam Hiyate of The Rights Factory read what I thought was my final draft and provided me with valuable suggestions and insights. Kathryn Sutton edited the manuscript, Michel Vrana provided the cover design and Laura Brady devoted herself to layout, design and digitization tasks.

Finally, I'd like to extend my deepest thanks to Caroline, my wife and my best friend, to whom this book is dedicated. Throughout our shared journey, you've helped me focus on what matters most. I love you!

Toronto and Snowmass Village

Spring 2025

Other works by Peter Cavelti

A Dangerous Remedy: A Novel
Breathtaking in its suspense and moral scope, "A Dangerous Remedy" is the story of Christian Unger's terrifying journey to protect his family from the psychotic wrath of his lover Claudia's ex-husband, David Talbot. As Christian confronts the frightening possibilities of David's vindictiveness, he's forced to cross moral boundaries and stumbles into a netherworld of brutal compromises where there are no easy answers, only survival. And murder.

A profound, highly readable meditation on the extreme measures we will take when the object of our love is threatened!

A creditable debut from an author whose moral message shouldn't be ignored.
—*The Globe & Mail* - Canada's National Newspaper

A morality thriller that questions the human impulse to categorize evil as a simple matter of villains and heroes. — Larry Gaudet, Author of *Safe Haven: the Possibility of Sanctuary in an Unsafe World*

An intense page turner that kept me guessing to the very end.
—Peter Plantec, Author of *Virtual Humans*

Tuiavii's Way:
A South Sea Chief's Comments on Western Society

Tuiavii, a young Chief in early 20th century Samoa, reveres the white man and his message of love. After all, haven't the missionaries taught his people to put down their weapons, honor one another and live in harmony? To visit Europe and learn its ways becomes Tuiavii's burning desire.

But once he arrives on the continent as part of a traveling show, he quickly becomes disillusioned. What Tuiavii witnesses is not the life of sharing and love he expected, but one in which greed, haste and hypocrisy dominate. Now he must find a way to return home and warn his people.

As delightful in their simplicity as they are prescient, Chief Tuiavii's comments confer the ultimate gift—the ability to see ourselves through another culture's eyes and, in turn, understand ourselves better. As we read on, we are saddened by the loss of simplicity and humanity in our society.

In his masterful translation, Peter C. Cavelti offers us Tuiavii's enduring wisdom, along with a cultural perspective, in English for the first time.

A fascinating and all too rare look at ourselves through another culture's eyes. Editor's Choice! —*Ottawa Citizen*

Profound and prescient, written from an innocent, yet enchanting perspective. — Publishers Group West

Recommended reading: a true eye-opener for all travellers to Down Under. —www.doAustralia.com, Australia's Tourism Website

A must read for any student of comparative culture and anthropology. — Roger Plunk, Author of *America's Highest Destiny*

★★★★★ Amazon.com

Moments In Time: The Experience of My Life

Peter Cavelti's three-volume memoir *Moments In Time*, both monumental and intimate, is a lifetime portrait that unfolds with the emotional depth of a seasoned writer. Cavelti starts off with his bourgeois childhood in rural Switzerland, relives his rebel years as a school drop-out, a confused soldier and a tormented immigrant in apartheid-era South Africa, before taking us on a backpacking adventure across Africa and Asia. Once in North America, he easily settles into Toronto's bohemian and corporate worlds and embarks on a most unlikely business career.

Adventure traveller, artist, corporate executive, philanthropist and, most of all, an empathetic chronicler of family life, Cavelti tells his story with psychological precision and a populist touch in presenting colorful characters from all walks of life – from cab drivers and bus boys, to mystics, artists and criminals, to world-changers in business and community life.

Whether writing about his own childhood, the joys and tensions under the surface of family life or the business world, Cavelti gifts us with an exquisitely rendered tale that captures the magic of relationships that matter amid life's uncertainties and challenges and celebrates the power of love in connecting us through our brightest and darkest moments. As a memoir, *Moments in Time* has the intricate honesty of a perfectly tuned Swiss watch – but one with a heart that beats powerfully on every page.

— Larry Gaudet, award-winning Canadian author

Thoughtful Giving:
A Journey Through the Charitable Universe

In this series of essays, Peter Cavelti shares the insights he's gained during his lifetime philanthropic journey. He provides practical advice on how to make sure that your gestures of kindness achieve the intended impact in the most timely, efficient and impactful way. Drawing on his experience as a small donor, an advisor to charities with global reach and community-focused organizations, and eventually managing a family foundation, he explains how you can be sure that your intentions are realized.

Includes valuable recommendations for individual donors and family foundations. Your gestures of kindness will not be in vain!
— Martin Hilb, Managing Partner of the International Center for Corporate Governance.

Thoughtful Giving combines grace, values, discipline and the gift of self. A perfect mix to turbo-charge the impact of your charitable giving.
— Steven Cornish, Executive Director, Doctors Without Borders

Peter's insights into how to give well are highly valuable to all donors, both big and small.
— Kate Bahen, Managing Director, Charity Intelligence